We'll Never Be Sixteen Again

At Sea

By

Mick Whitehead

For Sue, Craig, Harley and River
and all my family

Very special thank you to my editor
Paul Osman

This is the third instalment of the Mark Byrne Trilogy

Parts One and Two are available online
'If you haven't read these already, you're missing out on a lotta
rather good stuff.'

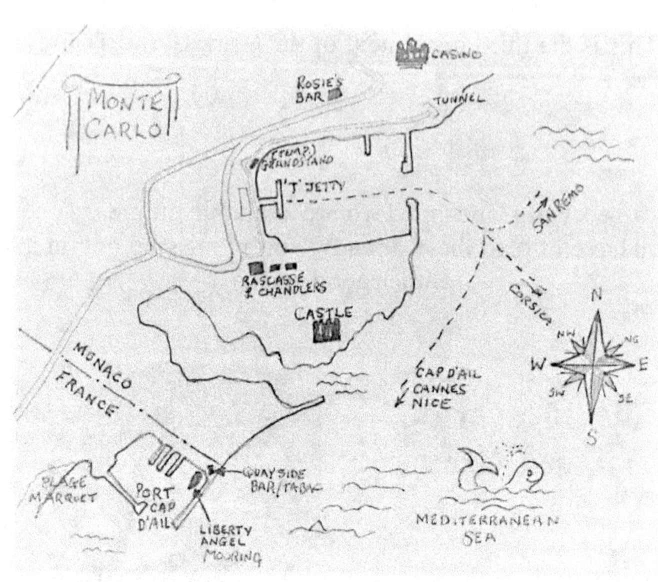

CASINO
MONTE CARLO
ROSIE'S BAR
TUNNEL
(TEMP?) GRANDSTAND
'T' JETTY
SAN RÉMO
CORSICA
RASCASSE CHANDLERS
CASTLE
MONACO
FRANCE
CAP D'AIL
CANNES
NICE
N
NW NE
W E
SW SE
S
PLAGE MARQUET
PORT CAP D'AIL
QUAYSIDE BAR/TABAC
LIBERTY ANGEL MOORING
MEDITERRANEAN SEA

ENGINE ROOM

Chapter One

The Liberty Angel

The days were beginning to feel warmer and my thoughts were drawn to the summer that lay ahead, the summer of 1977. It couldn't possibly be as hot, or as long, or as frantic as last year. A summer which in so many ways had changed my life. I thought about all the memorable, sweet times I'd spent with Max and working at the Friary and of course hearing Eve retell her incredible story. I had fallen for it all in a big, big way. My emotions had been brought to life and carried away on the wave of an inescapable rapture, no longer capable of feeling the ground beneath me. It had been an impossible dream. When Max died the dream died too and the flip side of it was facing up to the guilt of our actions. I vowed to myself that this summer would be nothing like the same. I was now a year older and if my emotional bruises were anything to go by, I ought to be a few years wiser.

By comparison, life on the French Riviera and in particular Monte Carlo didn't seem real somehow. I guess it was a form of escapism to be living in this sparkling, manicured resort which had been built specifically for pleasure, for wining and dining and soaking up the sun. If mum and dad could see me now, I thought, as I walked along the quayside, listening to the screams of joy from the large open-air swimming pool complex behind me. I studied the rows of exquisite boats and gleaming white yachts lined up, like a guard of honour to the rich and famous. This was the world I'd just signed up to. Was I mad, foolish, or just incredibly lucky? I guessed I'd find out in the coming months. In any case there were many worse places to spend a summer.

****

A warm haze of music and conversation hovered above a small, noisy crowd gathered on the fore deck. Each participant in the milieu had a least one bottle of beer in their hands: either a Kronenbourg 1664, or an Amstel, or both. In the background a casually attended ghetto blaster was sending out melodic waves into the lazy evening, around the tiny, French port. The work was well and truly done for the day. A shoal of mast lights, bound together, twinkled like stars and softly danced in the lap of the sea. A boisterous cheer rang out amongst the ships crew and their guests as a tall, wiry figure wearing a faded blue fisherman's smock jumped up athletically on top of one of the deck motors. With an air of authority he looked down on his audience with his arms outstretched, and then he lowered them gently to hush down the sound of the crowd. Captain Al spoke.

"Well chaps and chapesses, I'm just going to say a few words before you all get pissed and forget why you're here." This was met with a few agreeable cheers, which Al had deliberately paused for, but he'd not counted for a lone, drunken cry of 'get on with it'. Al glared at the foreign heckler, who had now taken refuge behind the broad shoulders of his mate, New Zealand Trev. Al continued, unperturbed.

"I would like to begin by saying well done everyone for getting this old girl of ours spruced up and ship shape for another season. From tomorrow, as you all know, we'll be leaving our winter moorings, here in Cap d'Ail." More hearty cheers rose up amongst us. "We'll be carrying out some sea trials and manoeuvres before we take up our new berth in Monaco. And, from then on, it's all about teamwork. Each of us needs to pull their own weight, meaning Trev's gonna be working twice as hard as young Byrney." More laughter. Al gently waved his hands out in front of us as he continued, above the semi-orderly decorum. "We need to remain focussed and to try and act professionally, for the next five and a half months."

Al changed his line of sight to individual members of the crew. "So, no clowning around, Dave. No throwing other people's deck shoes overboard, Gareth. No peeing over the handrail, Martin." A few giggles erupted. "Those of you who've been aboard last season will know exactly what I'm talking about. It's up to you guys to help out as much as you can so that we're all sailing from the same chart. There's no room for any soloists on the Liberty Angel." Al cast his stare at each one of us again, to emphasise his point. I was looking through a gap in the crowd at Magenta's face. It made me smile. For a cook, she looked more like someone set apart - bored, but very cool. She'd obviously seen and heard all this before.

"There's just one more thing for me to say," said Al, reaching out roughly in my direction, " and that is to wish a big Happy Birthday to Fionn." Fionn was stood next to me. A small, enthusiastic cheer rang out. "Come up here Fionn." Al lent down behind his feet and picked up a small, gift-wrapped parcel. Fionn was blushing very badly and bowing her head in embarrassment as she threaded her way forward. "A little something from me and the crew." Al handed over the parcel and smiled as Fionn stood awkwardly in front us. "Go on then, open it," he said, cheerfully.

Fionn carefully peeled back the coloured wrapper as a few wishful guesses from the back of the crowd were belted out in her direction, "It's a dildo!"

Fionn held up the bottle of perfume, Chanel No.5. Her look was a mixture of pleasure and relief. "Thanks guys," she said as she moved away from being the centre of attraction. I knew she never felt comfortable in those situations.

"Right, have a good night everyone and don't be late up in the morning." Al jumped down and disappeared into the Galley, closely followed by Magenta.

I went to join Fionn who was leaning with her back against the handrail, watching the rowdy activity resume as the music was cranked up once more and a plume of beer sprayed up into the air. These New Zealanders certainly knew how to party. Trev was one of the old hands. This was his fifth year aboard the Liberty Angel. A fact he liked to get into your face with, at every opportunity. He was built like a brick shit-house, so it wasn't wise to argue. Although he was just a deckhand, to all intents and purposes he was Captain Al's first mate. He kind of put the fear of god into me with his gung-ho approach to work. He was perfectly friendly enough, but there was a competitive edge to everything he did. He was very proud of his shiny, wooden handrail, which ran all the way around the aft deck. He'd given it at least three coats of clear varnish that I knew of and it shone like a mirror in the Mediterranean sunshine. He reckoned that the sterns of the yachts, lined up along the shoreline, were secretly judged by passers-by for their character and sparkle. "Look at the shine on that?" Trev had boasted yesterday, as he ran the palm of his hand over the rail. "Smoother than a monkey's bum."

Trev's biggest downfall, however, was the selection of hooligans he chose to befriend. He always made a B-line for his fellow countrymen, who were either holidaying, or beach surfing their way along the French Riviera on their annual pilgrimages. Tonight's raucous bunch was a typical example. I was thinking Captain Al had had the right idea by getting ashore for a quiet meal with Magenta.

Just at that moment, another loud cheer went up around the fore deck, followed by encouraging hoy-hoy-hoys as one of Trev's drunken mates, the very same one who'd heckled Al, had, of all things, mounted a bicycle. He was now doing a few laps, weaving in and out of the crowd. Where had that come from? His antics were attracting a lot of attention, mainly the wrong sort. I expected the owners of the small Bar/Tabac on the quayside next to us would be more than pleased to see us leave tomorrow. Under the glow of the moon, a few evening diners were sat quietly on its terrace, in defiance of the mayhem on board our ship. Not surprisingly, the drunken heckler soon began to lose control. The handlebars jerked violently from side to side and he crashed heavily into the steel gunwale. The impact caused the front wheel to buckle back like a slice of lemon and the rider flew over the front of the handlebars and over the rail. His handful of friends rushed to grab him, but fifteen feet below he hit the water before they could reach him. On the way to his splash down, the drunken heckler had let out a sickening groan when his head had struck and sprang back against the taught anchor chain.

Trev instinctively grabbed a life ring and threw it down to his friend, but there was no response. He was face down and unconscious.

"Bloody hell mate!" shouted Trev. He kicked off his shoes and without a second thought, jumped over the side. He held the head of his friend clear of the water and shouted up at us. "Somebody throw a bloody line down, quick!"

After a few frantic minutes and a lot of effort, for it had taken three of us to haul the body back over the rail, Trev swam around to the steps at the side of the aft deck and ran over the top deck and down the ladder again, back on to the fore deck. His mate was lying on his back in a pool of water. Trev, unprepared for what followed, was stopped abruptly in his tracks.

"There's nothing you can do for him Trev," said Gareth solemnly. "His neck's broken."

Fortunately, the diners at the Cap d'Ail bar had been spared this distressing scene as the drunk had gone over on their blind side, but within minutes the Port Police had arrived and were moving urgently along our gangway. They looked deadly serious, as if they were about to arrest everyone on board. They demanded to speak to the Captain, "Go and find him now, quickly, vite, vite."

If Fionn was cursed with attracting nutters and wierdos, I was beginning to think that everywhere I went in this world, the Police soon followed. I looked back at the dead body on the wooden deck and noticed Gareth had done the decent thing and covered it with his beach towel. I looked down at the face of Pluto, the Disneyland dog, smiling back at me. I didn't know whether to laugh or cry. I could see Fionn was shaken up by what had just occurred and suggested we went and waited in a quiet corner of the large saloon behind the galley.

"I guess you won't forget your seventeenth birthday in a hurry," I said. She didn't answer.

I'd hoped I'd not made the wrong decision by joining her here. For it felt to me, in the presence of the Police, as if it was also my 'liberty' which was under threat, once again.

****

"You'll love Captain Al, once you get to know him," Fionn had announced as we discussed our futures whilst sunbathing next to the Promenades d'Anglais in Nice, only two weeks ago. "Okay, so the pay isn't brilliant, but you'll get to meet a lot of interesting people and discover the sights of the Mediterranean. They say Corsica is a jewel worth seeing and the added bonus is all your accommodation and meals are free."

"Okay, okay. You've convinced me. Tell your Captain I'll come tomorrow, but seriously, what do I know about motor yachts?"

"It's not like school Byrney," teased Fionn, as she lifted up her sunglasses to flash her puppy dog eyes at me, "Mostly just common sense really, once you've learnt the basics."

I wasn't convinced it would be as easy as that, although I could tell Fionn really believed it was the right thing for me to do, instead of helping out at Patrice's printing studio. I knew Patrice was just being kind in allowing me to stay with him. Clearly, there wasn't enough full time work for two people.

"You make it sound like I've already been offered the job, Fi." I smiled back at her.

"Just make sure you're not late, that's all."

I'd taken the bus from Nice and jumped off at the sign welcoming travellers to Cap d'Ail. It was the last village in France before the border with the Principality of Monaco. I walked down the arid, sandy, winding path from the main road to the small marina. 'You can't miss the Liberty Angel. It's the last boat before the harbour wall,' Fionn had warned me.

When I reached the gang plank in front of the old fashioned, classic looking yacht, I wasn't sure what to do next. It wasn't as if there was a door to knock on, or a bell to push. I looked up at the top deck and could see the back of someone's head.

"Hello," I called.

I was beginning to feel a bit of a twit already, but I was quickly put at ease when the head turned around and said, "You must be Byrney. Step on board lad, I'll be down in a minute."

I gingerly walked across the floating gang plank and stood on the aft deck, under the pink stripes of a vintage, canvas canopy. The centre of this cool, shaded area had a large, round, oak table, which perched on a chunky, brass pedestal that was screwed to the deck. Around the edge was a circular bench seat with sumptuous, puffed up and buttoned cushions who's colour and style matched the canopy. For all their inviting comfort, I didn't feel like I ought to sit on them. Everywhere I looked, oozed luxury. The glass sparkled and the white, glossy paintwork drilled into the back of my eyeballs. I should have worn my Foster Grants. There was a smooth swishing sound as the saloon door slid open and Captain Al stepped out to greet me with an outstretched hand. He was much younger than I'd imagined, maybe in his mid thirties with a kind, unshaven face. I liked the look of him immediately.

Fionn had told me how he was a great storyteller over the daily evening meal with all the crew gathered at the table. Alan Smith had been a war baby and had never known his father. His absent father had been in the merchant navy before the war, mainly working out of Africa. He'd peddled and traded with the locals whenever he was ashore, swapping bars of perfumed soaps with the natives and in the same transactions relieving them of their tribal artworks - 'One day, he went to sea and never came back.'

Al was often asked by curious crew members if he'd wanted to track down his father? 'Not really,' was Al's stock reply. 'He gave me life and that was where his influence began and ended. My Ma always claimed he probably had a girl in every port.'

"Do you have a C.V?" asked Captain Al. I looked at him blankly.

"Curriculum Vitae?" he continued.

"No, we never did Latin at school," I replied.

Al smiled and said, "In that case tell me a little about yourself."

After inflating my experiences of school and working at the Friary, doing odd jobs and the like, Al asked me what I enjoyed doing in my spare time? I told him about my moped.

"So you know how an engine works then?"

"Yer, it's a two-stroke."

Al looked impressed. I think he was being genuine.

"We could use a handy person like you around here."

I hoped he wasn't expecting too much. I'd only ever changed a spark plug and adjusted the jet on the carburettor. It wasn't much and nothing at all to do with diesel engines.

He took me through the empty galley and out of a side door onto a small area of deck. From here there was a steel arched opening through into an inner gantry. Against the steel bulkhead were several nests of dials, switches and wheel valves. At the end of the short gantry were steel steps leading down to the dark depths of the engine room. My imagination conjured up a picture. For all I knew, the unfamiliarity of these strange surroundings could easily have matched the sandy stone steps of an Egyptian tomb leading to the mummified remains of old sailors.

At the foot of the steps, having switched on the overhead lighting Al proudly showed me the two large MAN Diesel engines. "They're submarine engines, as used by the Germans inside their World War Two U-boats." I think I was meant to be impressed, but mention of the war had taken me by surprise. I thought I'd left all that behind a few months ago in the Pyrenees.

I studied the two, sleeping, iron monsters and concentrated on my current surroundings again, forcing a smile.

"Do you reckon you can turn that wheel there?" he said, pointing at a large, spoked, brass rim at the end of the engine. I rested my hand on it and turned it from side to side feeling its weight and resistance.

"Yer, I reckon," I replied, optimistically.

"Good, there's nothing to be afraid of." Next, he pointed to a large, brass dial above my head. "That's the ships telegraph. It's how I communicate with the two lads driving the engines. Do you think you could work down here? It can get a bit hot at times."

I looked around and noticed how well organised everything was, which in a calming way made me feel confident. The tool cupboards were all complete and marked with a shadow system. There were hundreds of lagged lengths of pipework with more wheel valves of every shape and size, all tagged with a description for what they were used for or what they were connected to. Even the steel walkway was clean and free of any obstruction. The Portholes on either side of the room were just above head height, but if I stood on my tiptoes I could see the next boat, berthed beside us. It looked incredibly exciting. But it was beginning to dawn on me that I was feeling a bit of an imposter. What was I thinking? Up until now it had never occurred to me that I might fail or make a fool of myself or worse endanger myself and others alike.

But Al had a way of making the most complicated systems sound easy. "The ships a little bit like a lady, Byrney. Treat her gently and she'll purr back at you. There's plenty of life left in this old girl yet. Ready for a cruise around the Med?"

"Definitely," I replied confidently.

"Good Lad."

And that was it. Only twelve days ago, the job of engineer/deckhand/come jack-of-all trades became mine. As I was under eighteen years of age, I had to have a guardian's signature on my contract.

"Is that your old man I can see on the quayside?" joked Al, putting his hands up to shield his eyes. "Take this contract out with you this evening and when you bring it back tomorrow, if there's a signature in that space at the bottom, we'll say no more about it." He smiled and after shaking my hand, disappeared back into the lounge saloon.

Fionn said later, "don't worry about it. I forged my mum's signature on my contract too. No one will be any the wiser."

****

The Port Police had called for an ambulance to take the drunk's body away. The partying had long since died away too. New Zealand Trev was still sat making his statement to one of the Port Policemen, whilst Captain Al was talking to his opposite number of the dark blue uniformed variety. When he turned away, he came across to where Fionn and I were sat in the salon. Martin, Gareth and Dave had already joined us too.

"Bloody stupid bugger," said Al. "Bit of an inauspicious start to our season. Let's hope we can leave all this behind us when we set sail tomorrow." Al frowned, then slammed his hand down on the table, making us all jump. It was his way of snapping everyone out of it. "Come on," he said, "let's call it a night. I'll get Trev to tidy up his mess on the fore deck." We stood up together and watched one of the members of the Port Police wheel away the bent bicycle. He passed through the saloon and out onto the aft deck. It was the last any of us saw of it.

The atmosphere was still very subdued at the breakfast table the following morning. It would be our last meal sat altogether in the saloon for the next seven days. As from tomorrow, our first paying guests of the season were due to arrive, from the United States of America and from then on we'd be eating our meals out on the foredeck, if we were lucky. According to deckhand Dave, most of us would be just grabbing a bite to eat when we could, stood up inside the galley. Provided our guests had already eaten and provided we didn't get in Magenta's way.

Captain Al joined us, sitting in his usual chair at the head of the table. There was still no sign of Trev. I'd been fast asleep for a couple of hours on the bottom bunk the previous night, when I heard Trev stagger into the cabin, which we shared. As I was the last crew member to join, it was 'Hobsons choice' for me. The last remaining bunk was the one below Trev's, the one that no one else had wanted. If I forgot to roll over to make way for Trev climbing into his bunk, he usually stepped on my leg to lever himself up onto his mattress. If he carries on like this, I thought, one of these nights he's going to roll straight out of his bed. It was just wishful thinking on my part. In the unlikely event of any of our crew members leaving, it looked as though I'd be sharing with Trev for the whole season.

Captain Al looked around the table at the young, inexperienced faces in front of him as he lathered his scrambled eggs with tomato sauce.

"Cheer up you lot. It might never happen." There were a few half-hearted sniggers then Al turned to me. "Is Trev rousing yet, Byrney?"

"Still snoring away when I left."

"Martin, go and rattle his cage will you? We have to be making a move soon and we all need to look lively this morning."

Martin got up to leave as Magenta glided in with a fresh cafetiere of strong coffee. "You all look like you could use plenty of this," she said, lowering the large, enamel pot into the centre of the table and smiling at Al. I imagined she and Al were an item, thrown together by circumstance and the fact that they seemed so much more mature than the rest of us put together. Magenta had a knack of knowing what Al was thinking. I found myself staring at her again. There was definitely a certain mystery in the way she moved and her look was very striking. I was trying to work out if I ought to be afraid of her or not. Just for now, I settled for being wary. As she moved away with her back to me and sat down next to Al, I noticed her thick, black hair had been tightly pulled back and bundled together and held in place by a large, red, butterfly clip, revealing her slender, milky coloured neck. She poured her muesli into her bowl and looked up at me. I think she probably sensed I was staring intently at her. I moved my head away and nudged into Fionn.

"Hey, how much room do you need?" she joked.

"Sorry Fi."

We could hear Trev inside the galley, slamming the cupboard doors shut. He appeared in the doorway holding a carton of orange juice and then knocked back half of its contents.

"Woh, I needed that," he said, wiping the dribbles from his chin with the back of his mallet of a hand. "Got a mouth like a Maori's jockstrap." A few of us laughed. Magenta was not impressed.

"My apologies for last night guys," continued Trev as he sat down in the chair that Martin had vacated earlier. "Gee, I had a tough time convincing the Port Police I'd nothing to do with that dumb kid's accident."

I noticed Al rolling his eyes. He didn't look impressed with Trev either. "What time did they let you go?" he asked.

"Just after two a.m this morning, after they'd spoken to Neil's parents in Auckland."

"Gosh, that must have been awful for them," said Fionn.

"Yeh, I guess it was," sighed Trev. "Mind you, perhaps they knew something like this would happen one day. I only met Neil a few days ago and he was a right head case."

"Well, it's a Police matter now," interrupted Al. "Let's concentrate on the job in hand. I'll be coming round to see you all individually to run through the details of what we're hoping to achieve today." Al looked at his diver's wristwatch, holding up his arm for us all to see. "Two hours to departure, girls and boys." We took that as a cue to shuffle out of our seats and against the clatter of cutlery and dishes, I heard Al say seriously, "I'll start with having a word with you Trevor."

Martin was already at work down in the engine room when I joined him. He was busy tightening down the vent caps on the large bank of batteries that were housed beneath the footplates in front of the busy looking control panels. I helped him finish off. The batteries had been on charge for the past twenty four hours, so they were now fully charged up, apart from a couple of dead cells which hopefully wouldn't prevent us from firing up the engines when the time came. We screwed the footplates back down and moved to the next item on Al's checklist.

It was already twenty-two degrees centigrade inside the engine room and the permanent aroma of old engine oil and diesel clung to our blue boiler suits. We opened the four sea cock valves for the engine coolant. Then we topped up the diesel day tanks. Just at that moment, an alarm bell sounded at the top of the stairs, next to the opening onto the tiny deck area at the back of the galley.

"What's that?" I asked.

"It's okay, come with me," said Martin, "I'll show you." I followed Martin's confident stride up the metal stairway taking two steps at a time and pulling himself up on the handrail with both hands.

There were three gauges against the bulkhead by the little gantry at the top of the stairs. The one in the middle, marked Slurry Tank, was reading almost full. Martin pointed at the needle and told me to flick up the thumb switch directly below the gauge. The alarm stopped immediately.

"It's just a warning to let us know we need to empty the Slurry Tank. Normally we've got about half a day before it's completely full. Then the alarm bell will sound again until you empty the tank."

"Okay, I've got that," I nodded.

"What you mustn't do is empty the tank whilst we're moored up at the quayside."

"Why's that?"

"You'll see later," he laughed.

Al appeared from the rear entrance of the galley and was stood looking at us, with a smile on face. He was also wearing his captain's hat and a clean, white, short-sleeved shirt.

"I see you've shown Byrney where the alarm switches are, thanks Martin."

We all climbed back down the steps and stopped in front of the engines. Al quickly assessed how far we'd followed his instructions. He looked directly at Martin.

"Okay, so you checked all the oil sump levels, the day tanks. What about the generator?"

"We'll do that next," said Martin, blushing slightly.

"Okay, don't forget and don't forget the sea cocks on the genny too. I'll give you a shout when we need to start it, probably about ten minutes before we depart, should be long enough for the engine to warm up." Al rubbed his hands together and smiled. "Okay, choose your engine."

The two, big, black, silent monsters gave no clue to which one I should favour. They looked so old and still, I thought, how are we going to wake them up?

I put my hand on the port engine and said, "I'll take this one."

"Okay," continued Al. "We can't start the engines until we've cast off, the reason being both screws are direct drive. By screw, Byrney, I mean the propellers. Not the sort of screw you're thinking about. So, because our ship has no gearbox, as soon as the engines start, the screws start turning too and the old girl will try to move. So watch for the telegraph above your head. I'll ring down the command, then you move the engine according to my command and respond on the telegraph using that lever below it. Okay so far?"

"Yes," we both said firmly.

"The speed settings are here in front of you on the throttle ratchet arm. They're marked SLOW, HALF and FULL. To stop the engine, throw this red lever horizontal, okay?"

"Yes got that."

"Now, to set the engine in reverse you need to turn this big brass wheel anti-clockwise for a full turn." Al looked at us both and continued, "Okay, have a go. It won't harm anything. When you get to the end of the turn it becomes solid and won't go any further." We nodded in agreement. "Good, right, now a full turn clockwise until it feels solid again and we're back in the forward drive position." We turned our wheels back to their start positions, which took a little effort, since there was a resistance as the wheel turned. I looked across at Martin who was about half a turn behind me.

"Think I've got the awkward one," he moaned.

"Okay, that's most of it. Start you engines on your green buttons when I ring down. We'll probably head out to sea for about a mile or two. Then we'll stop engines and have a breather. I'll pop down to see how you're getting on. Any questions?"

Martin and I looked at one another and shrugged as Al reached up into a locker and handed us a pair of ear defenders.

"You'll need these, down here. And bring a bottle of water with you too. And if it get's a bit smoky, open both port holes."

Al caught the look of regret on our faces. "Don't worry, you'll be fine. Once you get used to things, you can stand on the little deck area at the back of the galley and get as much fresh air as you need." Al smiled, turned and headed back up the steps.

Martin went across to the other side of the engine room to check the generator. My first impressions of Martin were of his keen attitude and I liked the way he went about his work; he seemed very dependable. He'd spoken about how he wanted to make a career of working aboard motor vessels. He'd joined 'Liberty Yachts' in England, after responding to an advert for crew vacancies, in the magazine 'Yacht World'. He'd travelled to their head office for an interview in Barry, South Wales. They even paid for his fare from Bristol to the South of France, all be it by coach, probably the cheapest method. Up until then, Martin had been studying marine engineering at college. I'd noticed him referring to his text-books whenever he was alone in the engine room. I was anxious to put his mind at rest, that I wasn't a threat to his ambitions. If he wanted to be number one engineer aboard, that was fine with me. Despite his thoughtful silences we were getting along fine. And besides, he was a couple of years older than me, which also usually took a precedent where I was concerned. Right now, I was just happy to tag along for the ride.

After an hour, Gareth stuck his stubbly chin on the top gantry and shouted down for us to start the generator. Above the noise of the engine driving the genny, we could hear a few shouts coming from the aft deck.

"Sounds like someone's having fun," I quipped.

"You'd better look lively," replied Martin in his strong West Country accent. "Keep an eye on the telegraph."

All the lights and gauges on the control panels flickered.

"That's the shore power line being disconnected," he said. This was followed, immediately, by more shouting from up top and a loud, clunking noise from the fore deck.

"Sounds like the windlass has started. We must be weighing anchor."

I was about to make a funny comment, but thought better of it. I could tell Martin was looking slightly anxious as we both felt a slight tugging on the hull of the ship. Then suddenly both telegraphs sounded - Stand By.

"Here goes," said Martin as we both moved our telegraph dials to follow the word of command. Within a few seconds - Start Engines. Our fingers had been poised over the green buttons and the sound of rushing compressed air roared aloud.

Both engines fired into life at the same time in a slow thumping lethargic push, like someone being woken from a deep sleep. I noticed, in the corner of my eye, the mast of the boat in the next berth move slowly back past the porthole.

"We're on the move," I said excitedly.

Another command for both engines - slow ahead. The engines began to speed up and I was fascinated by all the exposed moving parts: the heavy looking crank, lazily turning and connecting rods and smaller push rods stretching up and down, all dripping in black oil. I'd better not go sticking my fingers anywhere near there, I thought.

Once we were clear of the harbour wall, the engines were set to half speed. The noise level had increased to the point where normal conversation was now impossible. The temperature began to rise and the air was starting to form a blue haze, which hovered around the overhead lighting. Martin opened his porthole and I thought it was a good idea to do the same. All that was visible through them was the clear blue sky, so it was impossible for us to see where we were in relation to the shore. I supposed we'd have to get used to not knowing.

After thirty minutes or so, Al rang down to stop engines. We waited a moment for further commands, but when none came Martin said, "come on, I'll show you how to empty the Slurry Tank."

On top of the small gantry, Martin opened a wheel valve, below the Slurry Tank level gauge. "Okay, all you need to do now is start the pump."

I found the button marked 'Start Pump', but nothing seemed to happen.

"Look over the side," said Martin.

I soon realised why it wasn't a good idea to empty the Slurry Tank whilst parked up in the marina. Apart from the obvious, foul smell of excrement, things of all shapes and sizes were popping up and floating on the surface, just below us.

"Look at the size of that one," I pointed, "must be one of Trev's." I'd not noticed Al appear behind us at that moment and he began to laugh too.

"Everything alright with the engines?" he enquired.

"So far, so good." I said.

The Slurry Tank alarm sounded again to indicate the tank was now empty and Martin silenced it and closed off the outlet valve. When he'd finished and turned around again, Al gave us a few new instructions.

"Okay, I'd like to practice a few forward and reverse manoeuvres out here, before we head off to our berth in Monte Carlo."

"Great." I said.

"Hopefully then, we won't hit anything expensive," he joked.

When we returned to the engine room I was glad we were going to be on the move again. Whilst being stationary, the Liberty Angel was rolling from side to side on top of the lapping waves, which was starting to have an adverse effect on my stomach. During our short practice manoeuvres, I could see Martin looked unhappy about the difficulty he had turning the wheel to set his engine in reverse and back again. I kept my eye on my telegraph to avoid watching him. There was no way I could help.

It didn't seem to take anytime at all to reach our berth on the 'T' Jetty in Monte Carlo. Once the engines had slowed and stopped, there were only two short commands for reverse before we were tied up on our mooring. After 'Finished With Engines', we eagerly ran up the steps to take a look at our new surroundings. Al came down from the Bridge to congratulate us, shortly followed by Gareth who had a broad grin on his face. "Wow! I couldn't believe it," he said. "We reversed straight in, in one go."

"Just like a handbrake turn," joked Al. "Pretty good for our first move, well done lads."

"Well, apart from dozy Dave," bemoaned Gareth. "He managed to drop the shore power line into the harbour at Cap d'Ail, probably blew one of their boards out at the port power house."

"We wondered what all the shouting was about."

I walked through the empty galley and through the saloon and out onto the aft deck, to get a closer look at our new neighbours. The late afternoon sun was as bright as ever. People in swimsuits were walking along the quayside, some just drifting by, admiring the line of yachts, others striding out with purpose. As far as my eyes could see most of the motor yachts tied to the shore looked brand spanking new: lots of sparkling chrome and luscious white leather seating and tinted windows, yachts flying flags of all nationalities. These yachts and the glamorous image they draped themselves in didn't appeal to me at all. The Liberty Angel, by comparison, certainly looked like the novelty ship in the harbour. At forty metres long, ours was probably the longest yacht fixed to the 'T' Jetty and looked slightly out of place. Because the Liberty Angel had been built in the 1930's, she was now considered a vintage vessel and as Captain Al had pointed out she had a pedigree that brought a certain nostalgia to the Riviera. It was this desire for the 'Golden Era' of the twenties and thirties, which attracted the rich and famous to charter our yacht, especially the Americans. Oh 'Tender Is The Night'.

Would they be impressed? Would we live up to their expectations? I guess we'd find out soon enough.

Looking up the quayside towards the castle, I spotted Fionn and Magenta carrying bulging bags of provisions slowly threading their way through the pedestrian promenaders. I hadn't realised they'd not been on board all day. Life was going to be very different for most of us from now on.

As I stood at the edge of the gang plank and absorbed the scene in fuller detail, I was awe struck with the beauty of the natural harbour. With the wonderful assortment of grand houses and hotels, stepping back in terraces in a perfect arc beneath the chalky, rocky summit of Mont Agel. It was an unforgettable sight. I could feel the hairs stand up on the back of my neck with excitement, but at the same time a niggling doubt lurked at the back of my mind that this adventure I'd attached myself to, could also be anything, but plain sailing.

Chapter Two

Entré Les Americains

"You guys are needed right now in the master cabin, aft," shouted Trev, urgently. He was standing at the top of the gantry, with his hands resting on his hips. I could tell by the look on his face he expected us to 'jump to it'. Our American guests had literally arrived less than an hour ago and there appeared to be some kind of emergency already - don't panic. Trev marched us to the master cabin and rapped his knuckles hard on the oak door. A man's muffled voice from inside replied, "Entrée," in a droll American accent. Immediately a picture came to mind of a smarmy, western saloon bar character, wearing a bootlace tie and a shiny waistcoat. Trev opened the door and announced, "two engineers for you sir."

Martin and I politely introduced ourselves and the big cigar, called Don, led us into the en suite bathroom and exclaimed, "there's a problem with the John - it's not working." After a silent pause and noticing our blank faces, he pointed at the porcelain pot to emphasise what he was referring to. I turned around and caught a glimpse of what must have been cigar's wife, walking through the doorway, on her way out. Pausing for a second she turned to her husband and said,

"I'll let you boys get acquainted. I'm going to get a drink, Don."

"Okay Marsha darling, I'll be right with you." Then, turning to us, Don the cigar gave us a big cheesy smile. I'd never seen some many white teeth in one mouth. "Well I'll leave you guys to do your job." For the next few minutes he fumbled about his half, unpacked case, which was still lying open on the grand double bed. I noticed on top of the centre of each fluffed up pillow was a ball of chocolate wrapped in golden foil – Ferrero

Rocher. Apparently, it was a traditional gift on board all Liberty Yachts for their guests each night. Not one of my favourites, I thought. With his back to us, Don rattled a few coins inside his pocket and then left, without uttering another command.

"So that's what a millionaire looks like," said Martin.

I tried flushing the toilet. The electric water pump struggled into life and the incoming water slowly pushed the water level higher, until it overflowed and spilled over the top of the rim onto the tiled floor. "Bollocks," I said.

Martin reached for one of the towels and made a dam around the base. "I don't believe this," he said, sounding very pissed off. "One of us is going to have to unblock the inside of the pan." I stared at the notice above the toilet with symbols of objects not to be disposed inside. "It's going to have to be you, Byrney."

"How come?" I asked.

"Because this sort of thing always makes me feel queasy."

I was about to put my hand inside when Martin leapt forward, "Byrney, wait! There's a macerator at the bottom, it'll take your fingers off. We'd better get some long nosed pliers."

As he scratched around inside his toolbox, I told him about me being on the wrong end of one of Gareth's practical jokes earlier. Just before our American guests had come aboard, I'd been cleaning up the last of the rubbish from inside the engine room and left it out on the poop deck, with the rest of the waste bags from out of the galley. (Strictly speaking, the small, enclosed, deck space, between the rear galley door and the arched entrance to the gantry above the engine room, wasn't a poop deck. We all called it that because that's where we left the poop). As I was about to step back inside the gantry, Gareth and Dave grabbed me. When I asked them what they were skulking about at, they whispered, "quick, inside here and watch."

"What is it?" I enquired.

"You'll see," said Gareth, smiling at Dave, who was also sniggering and struggling to suppress their secret. We hid behind the solid, steel, arched opening, on the gantry at the top of the engine room and waited for the rear door of the galley to open. "Have you noticed how Magenta enjoys dressing up?"

whispered Gareth. "It was her idea to wear a chauffeur's hat and gloves whenever she had to collect our passengers from the airport, kinky eh?" Just then the galley door opened and Magenta stepped out, right in front of us, turned to face the sea and removed her peak cap. Her hair unfolded slowly, spilling across her shoulder blades. She shook her head from side to side, tickling her bare skin.

"Every time," whispered Gareth, which set Dave off snorting and giggling.

Magenta turned around and frowned. "Who's there?"

I felt a hand on my back and before I could do anything to stop it, Gareth had pushed me out into the open.

"Oh, it's you," smiled Magenta. "Are you spying on me Byrney?"

I was struck dumb for the moment and felt the colour flush over my embarrassed face.

"Cat got your tongue?" She laughed and headed back into the galley. As she moved away, I was trying to work out what all the thin, exotic straps were for, that criss-crossed her back. When the galley door closed, Gareth and Dave re-appeared.

"You pair of sheisters," I half-heartedly complained.

"Hey, you have to admit, that was tasty. She does that every time. One of her little rituals."

"And was it tasty?" asked Martin, looking up from the flooded toilet.

I didn't have to think too hard for an answer. " Yes, it was."

"Well if you ask me, she probably knew you was there all the time," he laughed.

After another half hour of trying, we were still no further in unblocking the toilet. Captain Al had come to see what the problem was and suggested we would have to use the airline, to blow it clear with a blast of compressed air.

Al was stationed on the air valve at the top of the engine room and I was half way, relaying instructions to start and stop. Martin had the airline submerged inside the toilet and had taken the precaution of covering the outside of the loo with a bin liner, with just a small opening to allow access for the airline. For good measure, Martin was sat on top of the closed toilet lid, with his legs astride of the sinister looking block hose. "Okay, ready," he shouted.

I relayed the message to Al. No sooner had the air been turned on than I heard Martin yelling for it to stop. The airline relaxed again and I went to see the results. Martin was bent over the sink being sick. His legs were covered in thick brown freckles. There were more brown freckles on the bathroom floor too and along the side of the bath opposite and up the wall behind the toilet. Blimey, what a mess. I was trying my best not to laugh at poor Martin. When I lifted the lid of the toilet, all the water had disappeared and there, stuck to the underside of the toilet lid, was a pair of crumpled aeroplane tickets. I ran out into the galley to tell Al the good news. We'd cleared the blockage. I showed him the offending objects but he just scoffed, showing no signs of surprise. "You see all sorts in this game, Byrney."

"Think we're going to need a mop and bucket, it's a bit of a mess in there. And a few clean towels too."

"Okay, I'll get Fionn to bring it all down to you."

When I returned to the en-suite bathroom, Martin was still looking as white as a sheet. He had his hand over his mouth and was attempting to apologise for the additional mess he'd just made.

"Don't worry, Martin. I think you'd better get changed." Luckily, he'd been wearing his overalls, otherwise he'd be scraping lumps of brown stuff from off his skin. Or rather someone else would. Martin was in no fit state.

"I need to get a shower," he moaned and off he trundled.

When Fionn arrived, I tried to persuade her that I could manage by myself, but she insisted on helping and did most of the work herself.

"I can't believe they threw their plane tickets down the loo. Can't they read?"

"They probably have servants back home to do everything for them. What are our other guests like?" I asked, hoping they might be less demanding.

"They seem very nice. There's a tall chap called Roger, seems very quiet and then there's an older couple, Bill and Vivienne, who are lovely, but I don't care for Don's wife, Marsha. Have you seen her?"

"Not really, but I heard her jewellery rattling, when she went out onto the aft deck."

Fionn laughed. "Yes, at times like this, it does help to have a sense of humour, doesn't it?"

Poor Martin could do with one right now I thought. He was trying so hard to make a success of his job. Although Fionn hadn't gone into great detail about our guests, if the first hour was anything to go by, I had a horrible feeling they were going to give us the run around all week. But, hopefully, once they'd settled into their relaxed surroundings, then perhaps this would rub off on their attitude towards the crew.

As I carried the bag of dirty paper towels back through to the poop deck, I was stopped by Al, who was in the galley, filling his face with a door stop sandwich. "Everything cleaned up?"

"Yer, no thanks to the Yanks."

"Now, Byrney, don't forget these are paying guests. You have to make allowances for them."

His comments reminded me of working at the Friary and Madge and Edward, teaching me the politics of waiting on: "the customer is always right." Mind you, this didn't ever seem to play out when a customer complained about either of them two.

"How's Martin?" asked Al.

"He's looking very colourful, with his pale green face and brown legs. He'll live, but I can't see him joining us in here for dinner later."

Al laughed. "Worse things happen at sea, Byrney."

Not very reassuring I thought, as that was exactly where we'd be heading shortly.

From the crew cabins beneath the fore deck to our place of work was only a matter of half a dozen paces and mounting a short ladder into the glorious, Mediterranean sunshine. Even at eight o'clock in the morning and despite the fact it was still only early May, it felt intensely life affirming. And looking around at the scenery was a feast for the eyes too. I almost had to pinch myself to prove this was real. Here I was. To my right, taking command of the cliff top, was the historic Monte Carlo palace, home to Prince Rainier and his film star wife, Grace Kelly. And to think we shared the same view, albeit they were looking down on me and me up at them. But who cares, when the blotless, blue sky is reflected in the sea, announcing another incredible day. It felt like anything was possible and the trials of yesterday - instantly forgotten.

New Zealand Trev, however, I was finding a little harder to forget. He was fast becoming a real pain in the neck. I could put up with the constant teasing and name calling that bordered on bullying, but sharing a cabin with him I could easily have done without: in particular, the constant, noisy nightly interruptions to my sleep. He had the habit of slamming the door shut, every time he returned from his nights on the town. If he intended on painting it red, then surely by now the whole of Casino Square must be a deep shade of crimson. His favourite drunken tune, for some obscure reason, was Monty Python's Lumberjack song, followed by some of their familiar catch phrases: like, 'rather a lot really', spoken in a drunken, high pitched wail. Between the two of us, only Trev thought this was highly hilarious. Yet, more often than not, he was up and out of the cabin before first light. Perhaps it was just an unfunny phase he was going through, or the start of a losing streak.

The order of the day was obviously catering to the whims of our paying guests. As they were going to be having a guided tour of all the expensively famous sights of Monte Carlo with Magenta, Captain Al asked me to take a look at the tender. 'What's a tender?' I thought, but didn't say. I didn't want to appear too much of a 'yachty' novice.

"We've two tenders fixed to the upper deck," explained Al, as he walked over to a plastic looking, sit-up-and-beg type of small boat. It looked a little comical, like it could possibly have once been part of a fairground ride, albeit there was enough seating space inside for six adults plus the driver. It had a strong looking, snub nose, with a tall glass screen. Behind the uncomfortable looking plastic seating was a shiny Johnson fifty horse power outboard motor, attached to the stern.

"This is the Dory," he said. "We use it mainly for ferrying passengers to and from the shore. She looks a little odd, but she's very reliable and quite powerful too. She can even be used for water-skiing. As I continued to get acquainted, Al walked across to the opposite side of the deck and stood next to a wooden speedboat. 'Wow, this is more like it'.

The hull was built from narrow, tightly knitted wooden planks. It had a streamlined shape and was surmounted by a tiny, curved glass screen in a chrome frame.

"This, Byrney lad, is the Riva." Al smiled with pride.

"She's gorgeous," I said, calling it a she to make myself sound like I knew what I was talking about.

"Yes, indeed she is, but unfortunately we've not been able to take her out for quite a while." Al Frowned and continued, scratching his chin. "You know a lot about engines, don't you Byrney."

'Do I?' I thought. Apart from dad showing me how to check the oil and water of our car, I'd only ever tinkered with my moped and that was only ever changing a spark plug and adjusting the jet on the carburettor - hardly anything at all, really.

Al climbed inside The Riva and continued. "See if you can get her running?" He lifted the loose engine cover in the floor. "This is an inboard, Chevy V8 motor. What d'you think?"

I walked my eyes around the parts that I recognised: like the HT leads and the distributor cap and the centrally fitted carburettor, which sat between two slanted chrome covers, with the embossed lettering marked Chevrolet. Al turned the ignition key and the engine began rotating, coughing and spluttering, as if in protest. "I'll leave it to you Byrney," he said, optimistically. "If you do manage to get her started, don't run the engine for longer than a couple of minutes, otherwise she'll heat up without any sea water to cool her."

After five minutes of staring and wondering what to do, I was back down inside the engine room putting together a selection of spanners and screwdrivers and bits and pieces. When I told Martin what I'd been asked to do and how Al thought I was the man for the job, his only response was "best of luck with that, matey."

At least I was up outside, on the sundeck. If I couldn't fix the Riva, I could at least enjoy the view with the sun on my bare back. I stared at the slumbering engine, thinking that Al might have misplaced his faith in me. I knew I had to make a start, so I decided to stick to what I knew. I began removing the spark plugs, one at a time. I held the first one up to the light and examined its exposed tip. There were tiny specks of white powder stuck around it. I took my wire brush to it and gave it a good polish, before replacing it and moving to the next one. After half an hour, when all eight plugs had been cleaned I was quietly confident the engine would now fire, but sadly, no. I walked down to the empty galley, took a glass bottle of Coke from the fridge then climbed back up the steps once more, onto the sun deck.

'This isn't so bad,' I thought to myself ,whilst I waited for a tiny spark of inspiration to strike me. I looked back towards the tightly packed cluster of buildings along the sea front, observing the endless flow of traffic winding around the swimming pool complex and the lazy meanderings of passers by, nosying their way back and forth. It was kind of inspiring.

I returned to the problem of the slumbering engine - to my knowledge an engine required two, basic things: a spark and some fuel.

I removed one of the spark plugs again, fixed the HT lead to it and laid it down, on top of the engine cover. I watched the tip of the spark plug closely, to see if there was any blue flicker of light when I turned the ignition key - nothing, no spark. I traced the path of the HT lead back to the distributor cap and unclipped the two metal straps, to examine the inside. I noticed the tiny brass studs beneath each lead looked a little dusty, so I wiped them clean and did the same to the tip of the rotor arm, which I'd also removed. Whilst the cap was off, I turned the engine over again, to check for a spark at the points - nothing again. The points hadn't opened. That must be it, I thought. The arm of the points had worn down and the points were permanently closed. I flicked the ignition key on and off until the tiny cam on the spindle rested against the arm of the points. Hey presto, there was no gap in the points at all and therefore no spark. I was feeling really pleased with myself. All I had to do was adjust the base plate of the points to open up a small gap.

I'd watched my dad do this many a time. Running old bangers, as he regularly did, meant that he normally spent many an hour with his head stuck under the bonnet. Curiosity would get the better of me and I usually ended up standing next to him, passing tools to him and laughing whenever he got struck by one of the many, little, electric shocks. "Oo yer bugger," he'd say, shaking the electricity back out of his hand. "Pass me the feeler gauges." Of all the tools, in dad's wooden tool chest, these were the most intriguing. These tiny delicate fingers of steel formed a fan when they were opened out together. Each one was indelibly marked with a number. I knew by heart that number twenty-five was for the spark plugs and number fifteen was for the points.

I adjusted the gap on the points to fifteen one thousandth's of an inch and replaced the cap. I turned the ignition key confidently, but again nothing happened, not even a cough. Then I noticed the rotor arm was still sat on top of the engine cover. 'You idiot Byrney," I said out loud to myself.

With the rotor arm back in place this time the engine roared into life. It's powerful engine note purred like a panther. The unexpected noise brought Al rushing up to the sun deck, to congratulate me on my heroics.

"Well done Byrney," he said, sounding more pleased than surprised. I was surprised too, by how much having the Riva back in action had meant to the rest of the crew. I was the toast of the table when we gathered for our evening meal in the galley. I was candidly measuring their individual responses, which varied from Trev's 'you lucky bugger' smirk to Fionn's pride, Magenta's intrigue and Martin's tinge of jealousy. I sensed Martin felt I was making him appear inferior and that I was also taking away the opportunities he imagined for his own high ambitions.

Our meal was abruptly interrupted by a loud commotion, coming from the lounge next door. I could hear Marsha's grating accent, spouting off like a kettle that had been left on the boil. It was impossible to ignore. Al downed his mug of tea and went to investigate. We could hear all that was being said.

Marsha's diamond necklace had gone missing. Al was trying to calm her down, but Marsha was having none of it. Despite some plausible explanations from the other guests as to what might have occurred to them, Marsha was adamant. She had searched her cabin high and low and the only possible conclusion had to be that someone had stolen them and she was pointing the finger at "that waif of a cabin girl", Fionn.

We all looked at Fionn, who had begun physically shaking with distress.

"I wouldn't be surprised if she's dropped them down the toilet," I said in Fionn's defence, hoping for someone else in the galley to stand by her too. Gareth, to his credit, tried to divert the attention away from Fionn by asking if the jewels were insured, which raised a few eyebrows. In short, we were all stood together, in solidarity, whilst Al and Magenta carried out a search of the cabins.

When Al had finally satisfied himself that Marsha's crown jewels were missing, it became apparent that the only way Marsha would refrain from calling the police and remain aboard would be if Fionn was removed immediately. There was no way Fionn was capable of such blatant thievery. I told Al so. I'd known and worked with Fionn for a long time. She was the most honest person I knew - too honest for her own good it seemed. She was in floods of tears as she was lead away, accompanied by Magenta, who'd volunteered to taxi Fionn back to Nice.

I felt sick to the pit of my stomach. I could very easily have walked away in protest, but where would that have got me. Captain Al spoke cautiously to the rest of us, later. Of course, we should keep our eyes out for any sign of the jewels. When

Al had reluctantly searched for them in Fionn's room, there was no trace of them there, or anywhere else for that matter. But Marsha had been quick to point out that Fionn could easily have smuggled them ashore at any point during the day, whilst everyone had been preoccupied with gallivanting around the sights of Monte Carlo.

Later that evening, when I was alone with Al, I asked him if he thought Fionn had taken the jewels.

"It doesn't matter what I think," he said. "What matters most is to keep our guests happy for the reputation of Liberty Yachts. It's just business, Byrney. But, for the record no, I don't think Fionn took them for one minute. If all goes well for the rest of the week, we'll be able to bring Fionn back, when the American's have left.

The next morning I was hoping I didn't have to cross Marsha's path. I wasn't sure how I would react to seeing her again. But the Liberty Angel's course was set for Corsica and the demands from down inside the engine room meant my mind was kept fully occupied. Martin and I were getting along well together as a partnership. I was allowing him to take the lead in choosing the tasks that he preferred to do, even happily taking orders from him. As the ship pitched back and forth in the lap of the waves, it felt like we were sat on the fulcrum of a see-saw. We stood with our legs astride, pretending to add our weight to the rocking of the boat.

The first thing we noticed that showed the sea around us was becoming rougher, were the tiny splashes of sea water being deposited through the engine room portholes. Then, suddenly, the ship pitched forward into a nose dive. It felt as if some giant sea monster had literally lifted the stern of the ship above the water line. The whirring screw suddenly sounded several notches louder as we both fell back against the workbench. The angle of the floor fell away and the whole ship juddered to a momentary halt. It was an awful sound. Even the floorplates beneath our feet lifted up, revealing a dark, slimy liquid and a watery grave. As we recovered our balance, we heard a storm raging inside too, glasses smashed and pots crashed. The telegraph rang down from the bridge, ordering us to slow down to half speed. Wave after wave whooshed as they struck against the side of the hull. From inside the engine room, they sounded like the ghostly echoes of the rapid rifle shots from a firing squad. This storm had risen up from nowhere, carried along by an ominous 'Mistral'.

We had set sail in such heavenly, calm waters but twenty miles out at sea and we were now in the lap of the gods. We pitched forwards violently once again, but this time we were ready for it and we clung on to something solid. Then the ship rolled over one way, then the next, lolling submissively. I found myself subconsciously wondering how long each roll would last until the ship sprang back the other way again. This was far more scary than being stuck in the snow, whilst descending from the summit of the Col du Monde. Falling from a great height, I calculated, would be an infinitely more pleasurable end than the imminent prospect of being dragged down to the depths of Davy Jones Locker, trapped inside a submerged motor yacht. It reminded me of a junior school friend, Nige, who was learning to swim at the same time as I was. The swimming instructor had enquired how far could he swim? "All the way to the bottom," he'd replied. "Is that far enough?"

Captain Al appeared at the top of the gantry looking anxious with his hair all dripping wet. I could see he was genuinely pleased to find us both in one piece.

"Alright down below?" he yelled. We gave him the thumbs up.

"We're going to have to find some shelter. By my reckoning if we head due west we should find a cove at Agnello Point. Just hang on in there for another hour and we should be through the worst of it." He waved at us and disappeared.

"I don't know about you," said Martin, "but I'm going to put on a life jacket."

"That's the most sensible thing you said all day," I joked, trying to lighten up our fears.

Whilst Martin went to the muster point locker, I checked that the engine room port holes were firmly closed.

Ten minutes later, this time it was Trev who appeared at the top of the gantry, with two mugs of tea in one hand. For once, we were both pleased to see him. He began laughing at us, cowering in our yellow cork vests, as he descended the stairs. "Look at you pair of wimps. Here take these?" I looked inside the mugs. It wasn't tea; it was rum. I mentioned that some of the portholes inside the forward cabins might still be open. Trev glared at me, knowing it was my responsibility to see to the one in our cabin.

"You'd better check them all just in case?" I ventured.

Trev was enjoying every moment of our discomfort. "Bloody typical," he said. "Whenever the shit hits the fan, it's good old Trev to the rescue." And with that, he leapt back up the stairs, striding them two steps at a time.

Al's hour of reckoning passed slowly, for it seemed like the storm was relentless. I tried to imagine what the galley floor must be like. We could hear all kinds of noises rolling about above our heads and to the accompaniment of unattended cupboard doors, constantly slapping open and shut. The only consolation I could find for myself was at least I wasn't paying thousands of dollars for the privilege, unlike our poor, rich guests.

When the cool light formed in the early hours of the following morning, we were lying in calmer, shallow water, surrounded on three sides by indistinct, lifeless rocks. Out beyond the cove the distant sea still roared. It appeared to be covered by a thick band of white foam. The prospect of the whole day looked and tasted of boredom. It was a day spent cleaning up the mess and surveying the damage and someone (thanks Magenta) was having to feed and entertain the guests. Americans, we discovered, loved their cocktails and by mid afternoon they were all staggeringly drunk and retreated to their cabins.

"What's the damage like?" enquired Al on his long awaited visit to the engine room. Martin had managed to retrieve all the spanners and tools from the shadow boards and I was making sure the day tank on the generator was topped up with fuel. Al was looking a little stretched and tired. He told us that he and Trev had shared the watch during the night. The wind had ceaselessly tried to drag us onto the rocks, at times even dragging our anchor along the seabed. I mentioned to Al about seeing the footplates lifting up and that I thought I saw water swimming around beneath them.

"We'd better take a look at the inspection hatches." Al lifted one of the steel plates at the rear of my engine. Quite clearly there was an alarming amount of seawater inside the bottom of the hull.

"It's only to be expected," he said reassuringly. "We'll run the bilge pumps for an hour, that'll soon have it bailed out. Nothing to worry ourselves about for now."

The overall smell inside the engine room was quite nauseating. Martin was looking decidedly sick again. I couldn't help but feel sorry for him.

"Let's get some fresh air for a while."

The day continued to feel as empty as our appetites. We watched a lone grey seagull skim across the surface of the grey sea, complaining as it swooped over our bow in the grey sky set like the reverse side of a canvas.

Day two of our confinement was an exact replica of the previous afternoon, except during the night we must have been joined in our enforced sojourn by another vessel. The dark grey sinister shape was moored about one hundred yards away to our stern. It was too far to notice if anyone was standing on its deck. Its anchor chain was held taught at forty-five degrees.

Al was busy on the radio set, alone in the small bridge house at the front of the upper deck. He was trying to get a reliable weather report. Once again we were unable to budge. Once again the restless guests complained, drank themselves into a stupor and complained again. The one thing that got to me the most about them was how loud their voices were. They didn't care for private conversations and Marsha was obviously their self- appointed ring leader. There wasn't an ounce of her that I cared for.

Being stuck in one place for too long wasn't good for the crew's morale either. Trev was becoming ever more vindictive and cruel. Bored of his name calling in my direction, he'd begun to switch his attention towards Magenta.

"You're just a Sheila. What do you know about anything? All girls are good for is cooking and doing the dishes."

Magenta never let her feelings show. We all saw Trev was doing his best to goad her at every opportunity, but Magenta was far too cool for him to understand.

After the last meal of the day, Trev had finally gotten a response from her. He'd challenged her to an arm wrestle.

"He's a cruel bastard," said Gareth, out of earshot, "I wish someone would teach him a lesson."

As I watched Magenta lean into position opposite Trev against the working top, I couldn't understand why she'd agreed to take Trev on like this. Physically she was no match for Mr. New Zealand. They placed their elbows together and locked hands. Trev was wide-eyed and raring to go. He couldn't wait to put Magenta in her place. It was a valiant attempt on her part to avoid defeat. We all saw Magenta's resistance was quietly and defiantly brave. Trev was so focussed on victory he'd failed to notice her unflinching smile.

"Best of three?" exclaimed Trev, buoyed by his success as Magenta's air of resistance had apparently caved in.

"Actually I have a challenge for you," she replied. "Wooden Spoons? Have you ever played wooden spoons, Trevor?"

I wondered what Magenta was up to. I saw Gareth smile and move behind Magenta who was now standing with her face almost touching Trevor's. "Or aren't you man enough?"

"Sounds a bit girlie if you ask me, but alright then. What do I have to do?"

The challenge involved both combatants sat facing each other. The first person to strike held a wooden spoon in their mouth and by lifting their head they brought the spoon crashing down on their opponents head, whilst essentially maintaining a grip of the spoon with their teeth clenched upon it. Their opponent wore a tea towel over their head for protection, which also covered their eyes whilst they sat in the dark, anticipating the blow.

Trev was eager to have a try. Magenta covered her face and Trev with hands behind his back awkwardly managed to strike Magenta's head with only the force of a flea. He hadn't quite mastered the art of gripping his wooden spoon tight enough.

Now it was time for Trev to cover his face.

"Are you ready Trev?" enquired Magenta.

"Sure, do your worst," he said, cocky confidently.

Magenta placed her spoon between her teeth and nodded to Gareth. From behind his back a rolling pin suddenly appeared and he tapped Trev's cranium with it, quite fiercely, making the sharp sound of a lovely, solid clunk. We all raised our hands to our mouths and held our shoulders as hard as we could to stop them from shaking with laughter. With the rolling pin swiftly hidden from view again, Trev had no idea what had happened.

"I can tell there's obviously a knack to this, let me try again." he tested the strength of his grip on the spoon by practising jerking his head.

Magenta graciously donned her towel, but again the strike from Trev was woefully feeble. He took a deep breath and folded his tea towel in half.

"Hey, no cheating," replied Magenta quickly. Trev unfolded the towel and once more braced himself. This time Gareth struck even harder than before and Trev hissed in pain. I could almost detect his eyes rolling around from the back of his head as he whipped the towel away to see Magenta facing him with her spoon still tucked inside her mouth.

"Bloody hell, that hurt," he complained, rubbing the tender area. But the pain only spurred him on into having another go. We all looked away to hide our giggles. "What's going on?" complained Trev, sounding slightly annoyed.

"Nothing Trev, honest," I said.

Trev tried again, through sheer frustration, but it was still far too feeble. No one could now believe that Trev was going to fall for it a third time. The rolling pin accurately struck at exactly the same spot on Trev's head again. This time he flung his towel down to the floor and stormed off. "I've had enough of this crap." As soon as his back was turned, we all fell about laughing hysterically. He'd still not twigged what had happened. Magenta looked at me and raised her thick dark eyebrows. I could tell she was thinking exactly the same as me. It was a sublime moment.

Chapter Three

Corsica

The weather report finally came through to Al with some good news, and at exactly midnight we were slowly on the move at last, inching further down the coast with our Port and Starboard lights glowing brightly. There was no way we could allow our guests to wake up to the same boring view as they had the previous two days. They were already over half way into their week's charter and so far, all they had to show for their venture was a half-day tour around Monte Carlo. Fionn would be pleased; so far she'd not missed a thing.

A clear blue sky greeted them when our guests awoke and they were able to take breakfast in the luxurious ambience of the aft deck. Indeed, it was the first occasion they'd all been able to dine aboard 'al fresco'.

For the crew, there was a marvellous smell too: of eggs and bacon, calling us and leading us up to the galley for a well earned breakfast.

It had been a late night for most of us. We hadn't anchored until three o'clock in the morning, when the clear, starry sky was starting to dissolve into the ochre tones of sunrise. In the early dawn waters, around the bay of Porto Vecchio, on the east coast of Corsica, we'd just enough time to stand on the fore deck and admire the distant lights before heading down to our bunks. The Liberty Angel had come to rest when Captain Al laid out three to four lengths of anchor chain and piloted her slowly astern, until he felt the anchor bite on the seabed. Martin and I waited for the final command - finish with engines.

As we stood there in the stillness, on the wooden deck, a warm welcoming breeze glided across the inky pool between the ship and the shore. Our thoughts, as ever, were racing forwards.

"Looks very inviting," said Martin, pointing towards the town. "Hopefully, we'll get a chance to go ashore sometime tomorrow."

"Yer, I can't wait." This is what it's all about, I thought.

"Goodnight Byrney." Martin headed below and I took one final glimpse at our new situation. I could hear Al and Trev behind me, up in the wheelhouse, discussing the day's plans for our guests.

A few hours later, I'd woken to the sound of the hatch sliding open on the fore deck. It was the usual signal that some of the other crew members were already out and about. I listened to the sea slopping against the side of the hull. It felt strangely comforting. Much like listening to the rain beating down on our caravan tin roof with a warm duvet to snuggle up to.

It would have felt nicer still, here in our tiny cabin, had Trev not been snoring like an old tramp.

Which made me think. There used to be this old sad sack of a guy who tramped the streets back home in our town. His name was Cody and we'd sometimes see him, when we cut through the park, on our way home from school. He would be sat on a small hump of grass, with all his possessions of a lifetime scattered before him. I'd never seen anyone wearing so many clothes at once, even in summer. He never spoke when we passed close by. He just lowered his head and his thick white whiskers would bend over his chest, with his gaze fixed on the flapping soles of his shoes. We made up stories about him, about how he was really a millionaire, but was unable to cope with his wealth. I wondered about all he must have seen, the daily comings and goings that we were hidden from, tucked away in school seven hours a day. Then, quite unnoticed, Cody just seemed to vanish, bundles and all. I remember mum telling us sometime later that he'd been set upon and beaten up by a gang of youths. Why is it that the most vulnerable and harmless are singled out in this way? As if he hadn't already suffered enough.

As we were tucking into our breakfast, we all began to laugh when Al enquired, "That's a nasty looking lump on your forehead, Trev." The silence was golden. Dave, being slow on the uptake (about two days behind on this occasion) asked, "Was that one of the worst storms you've sailed in Al?" To be kind to Dave, I recognised his ploy. He was tactically hoping to get Al meandering with one of his long-winded ocean tales, in the hope of delaying the start of the day's workload.

"Aye, it was a bad tempered wind, that's for sure," agreed Al, looking round at our bemused faces. "Those Mistrals can soon whip up a force nine or ten in the Bay of Lions. I've seen it many a time, especially when they're funnelled through a mountain gap. They can even pop up right out of a clear blue sky. You can't take nothing for granted in the Mediterranean, one minute the sea's as smooth as glass, then the next... well you all saw what happened. It can catch out many a novice sailor." Al took a sip of his coffee. "It was a similar storm to the one we had two days ago that did for poor Percy Shelley," said Al discerningly. We all looked back at him dumbfounded.

"Percy who?" said Dave

"Shelley, the poet, Ozymandias? Blimey what did they teach you lot at school?" he enquired. "Well, Percy was living beside the Riviera and longed to have his own boat. He even helped design it himself. Anyway, he and a friend took her out on her maiden voyage, on a day very similar to this one: bright blue skies, gentle, westerly breeze. His boat got caught up in a bad tempered Mistral that only lasted around half an hour. But, it was still just long enough to capsize his boat and send it to the bottom. They found Shelley, about a week later, washed up about forty miles further down the coast. They only identified him because he kept his book of poems in his jacket pocket.

They built a funeral pyre for him right there on the beach. And that was the sad end to young Percy."

"So when did all this happen, Al?" probed Gareth.

Al rubbed his chin, "Around 18 ... 25"

"What, twenty-five past six last night?"

"The year 1825, you dummy." Al clapped his hands. "Right come on then, back on your heads." Which was Al's way of saying jump to it. "Lucky for you lot you've got the benefit of my experience at the helm."

"Who's Ozzy Mantis?" asked Dave to no one in particular as we went out separate ways.

"He's that bloke who prays a lot," kidded Gareth.

My and Martin's plans for getting ashore for the day were scuppered, by some urgent repairs to the ship's twin screws. If we were to avoid a repeat of the bilges filling up, we had to find how and where the seawater was leaking in from. When we lifted the inspection covers and bilge plates under the engine room again, there was another sizeable amount of seawater, staring menacingly back at us.

Al took a deep breath and said "Let's take a look aft." As we climbed out on deck into the warm sunshine, I noticed the Dory had been lowered down alongside and the Americans were descending the short, wooden steps. Gareth was helping them into their seats. 'Lucky buggers,' I thought. Al led us into the aft cabin. At the end of the passageway was a steel door, with a sign above it that read: Crew Only - No Admittance.

Al unlocked the door to reveal a gloomy, bow-shaped cave. It had just enough room for the three of us to stand in. Beneath our feet were two more inspection covers. Beneath each of them lay the thick, shiny, steel shafts that ran fore to aft. At the point where the shafts exited the stern there were two chunky square flanges, secured by a circle of retaining nuts.

"Okay chaps, get your spanners ready Martin. Right, you both need to climb down into the bilges, and what we're going to do is to try and compress the gland packing, in those flanges."

We looked into the bottom of the bilge. The depth of water held no clue as to how far our bodies would be submerged. I looked at Martin and said, "after you."

"Well, come on chaps. There's nothing alive down there," barked Al.

We removed our yachty shoes and lowered ourselves into the cold, slimy liquid. My feet touched the rough solid steel floor just as the water level crept up above my knees. At this very moment, I wasn't feeling all that comfortable. Instead, I was thinking of all the dirty, horrible jobs Edward had got me doing at the Friary, but they weren't even close.

Al was keen to emphasise that it was essential, not to tighten up the gland housing too much. If we completely closed the gap between the two flanges then no further adjustment could be made and we'd have to remove the flanges all together. This could only be done in dry dock, he told us.

Al passed down the spanners and suggested we linked a ring spanner and an open-ended spanner together to get more purchase and leverage. "Either of you seen the film 'The Cruel Sea'? One of my favourites," boasted Al. "There's this dramatic scene where the escort vessel is afloat like a sitting duck, waiting to be torpedoed as the engineers replace a shaft bearing. Big job it was. The crew were all sat on pins." Al began wooing like a ghost. "Then the chief engineer strikes his wrench with a lump hammer, sends an awful noise ringing out all over the ship and one young lad whispers, 'if the Gerrys don't get us now they never will."

"Sounds fascinating Al," I said, bemoaning the state of my slime covered legs. "All done and there's still about a half inch of gap. That's as tight as I can get it."

Martin had already climbed out and was wiping the black sludge from his legs.

"Stay here, I'll get a couple of towels." As soon as Al had turned away I asked Martin how much he enjoyed being an engineer right now. But I didn't need to hear his reply. I could see how pleased he was, being useful and making a success of it.

"It'll soon wash off," he said, in his broad, west country twang.

'That's chuckle butty,' I thought.

We carried our shoes through the empty lounge. Magenta and Dave looked round, smiling sympathetically, as we passed through the galley and out onto the poop deck. The sun was high in the cloudless sky, which warmed our moods. We could hear bathers on the distant beach, paddling and splashing, close to the edge of the gentle rush of the breaking waves.

"Come on, lets get cleaned up. Maybe Al will let us go ashore now this evening?" There was a loud splash in the water beside us. Trev had jumped off the fore deck and was taking advantage of having some free time.

"That's Trev for you," grumbled Martin. "He's a bloody show-off."

I wasn't listening. My mind was elsewhere. I was thinking about what everyone else was doing right now: Anna at college in America - Mum, dad and Anthony back home - And poor Fionn back in Nice. No doubt Henri and Juliette would be taking care of her. I really hoped her absence from the Liberty Angel was only temporary. The Liberty was missing her angel.

Gareth was handling the Dory skilfully as he drew up alongside. He put the gearbox in neutral and held the bottom of the ladder as we stepped aboard. I was quite impressed by just how powerful the little outboard motor was. The nose of the Dory rose up sharply when Gareth gunned down on the throttle, whilst simultaneously twisting down on the little steering wheel and we accelerated away, in the direction of the Marina di Porto Vecchio. It was my first time on a speedboat, but I wasn't sharing that fact with anyone. Every once in a while, I was still having feelings of being out of my depth, of not belonging. I put it down to nerves. It only occurred to me when I thought about it. No one actually said it to me. In fact, with the exception of Trev, I'd been accepted instantly by the other crew members.

As soon as we were moored up, speak of the devil himself, Trev leapt impatiently onto the quayside, with a wave of his hand. It was no surprise to the rest of us that Trev went his own way. For me, it was a relief to get away from him for a couple of hours.

We moseyed up the ancient, narrow streets. There was only a narrow path down the centre for us to walk along, as the tables and chairs from the bars on opposite sides almost cut off a way through. The atmosphere was alive with the buzz of a hundred conversations amongst the drinkers, posers and promenading passers by. We walked past table after table of diners, gorging on mussels and fish. The wooden framed entrances to some of these bistros were bedecked with octopus, hung out to dry in the daytime sun.

"So people actually eat those?" I asked.

Magenta looked back at me and smiled, "there's a lot worse than that: turtle steaks, squid, urchins and sea slugs…"

"Okay, I get the picture," I said, waving my hand. "Don't spoil my appetite."

We found a nest of empty tables at the Bistro 'Fruits de la Mer' and after studying the menu and knocking back a cool demi of beer, it was swordfish for me, please. It might stand me in good stead to have a sword inside my belly when it came to defending myself against Trev's usual, intrepid, drunken arrival in the early hours.

I was enjoying being a small part of this wonderful street banquet. It was a perfectly warm evening and my shipmates were all cracking jokes and talking shop, or in this case talking ship. Gareth had been telling us about when he'd dropped the Americans off earlier and how, as soon as they set foot on dry land, they began falling out with one another. In the end, Marsha had got her own way and the rest of the party were last seen trailing behind in her wake, as she headed towards the fashionable boutiques. She was in desperate need of some retail therapy, having been cooped up on That Damn Yacht like the bedraggled ancient mariner. At least she was out of earshot this evening.

When we returned to the quayside and clambered back into the Dory, there was no sign of Trev.

"Well, we're not waiting for him, he'll have to make his own way back." grinned Gareth.

Al had insisted on us returning aboard early, before our guests, in case there was some 'un catered for' whim that had slipped past them on their return. I watched Magenta preparing cocktails in the galley. She was reading from their nightcap order that they'd left out: four Gibsons and a Stinger. Let me guess who was having the Stinger?

I was just dropping off to sleep. Anna and Max were both arguing about which of them was going to share my bunk this hot night, when suddenly, the cabin door slammed shut, followed by that dreaded, drunken slurring. Trev was back. I switched on my bulkhead light, before he broke any more of the furniture.

"I see you made it back then?" I sounded just like my mum.

"Bribed one of the locals to drop me off," came the drunken reply.

Pity he didn't drop you half way, I thought. I am turning into my mum, just the sort of thing she'd say to dad.

The drunken voice piped up again, "Byrney, I need fifty Francs for the pilot. I sat up. I couldn't believe I was hearing this.

"What happened to the hundred Francs I lent you last week and the hundred the week before?"

"You cheeky sprog. You'll get it back as soon as I get paid." It was bad enough putting up with this drunken routine almost every night. Enough was enough, I thought.

"No way Trev. I can't keep giving you my money." Trev suddenly stood up straight and looked around the cabin. I thought he was going to hit me with something.

"Okay, proposition for you," he garbled, raising a finger and wobbling his hips to maintain his balance. "Give me another hundred Francs and you can have my ghetto blaster, then we're straight. Wipe the slate clean and all that. Deal?" He held out his right arm to shake hands. I looked at Trev's Phillips

Radio/Cassette player, with twin speakers, and after a few, momentary misgivings I accepted.

"Okay, pass it over." I retrieved my wallet from the hidden, zipped compartment in my rucksack and handed over two, Fifty Franc notes. "This is the last time, I mean it." Trev stared back at me from under his heavy lidded eyes. You never knew with Trev if he was going to strike out at any second, or not. His body hadn't tensed up at my last comment, so I guessed he'd accepted. I watched him stagger out of the door to pay the ferryman. Ten to one he'll forget about our deal come morning. I hid the ghetto blaster inside my rucksack, hoping that out of sight meant out of mind.

Full ahead on both engines the following day, as we skimmed the tops of the waves at a flat out speed of eleven knots. I relayed to Martin what had occurred with Trev the night before. Martin blushed as he admitted that he should have warned me about Trev.

"He's notorious for it, borrowing money from the rest of the crew. He's done it with everyone, well all except Al."

Martin turned away and began filling in the daily, engine room logbook. We were heading around the southern tip of the island and back up the west coast: destination Ajaccio, the capital of Corsica. Distance from Porto Vecchio was roughly eighty nautical miles. Martin recorded the hourly reading from both engines: temperature, oil pressure, speed etc.

"Should take us about seven hours or so," Martin shouted. I nodded back at him.

The sea was calm enough to have both the engine room portholes open. The cool breeze helped to disperse the blue haze above the noisy, iron monsters, which propelled us along. We were both wearing our ear defenders, which did little to drown out the din, so conversation was very limited between us. I raised a finger to Martin to indicate I was going up top, onto the poop deck for a respite from the fumes and the noise of course.

Leaning against the handrail with my head stuck out to face the oncoming breeze I uncovered my ears, to listen to the music coming out of the galley. Magenta usually had a cassette on the go when she was busy working. I tuned into the track she was playing which sounded really summery and upbeat. It was like nothing I'd heard before and I had no idea who it was. The lead vocal alternated between a woman and a man. I stuck my head around the corner and saw Magenta chopping and slicing away, which looked quite dangerous so I waited to catch her eye before calling out. Magenta frowned at my unwanted interruption.

"Sorry I..."

"What do you want Byrney," she said, lowering her knife.

"I just wondered what this music was, you're listening to? I really like it." Why do my words always seem slightly naff, I thought, when I'm trying to sound cool - If only...

Magenta's frown relaxed into a smile. "It's Fleetwood Mac's new album, Rumours. You can borrow it later if you like." The only Fleetwood Mac song I knew was Albatross, and this sounded nothing like. Maybe they'd hung the albatross around Marsha's neck. I ducked back out of the way, with a thumbs-up to Magenta. With nothing to see but wave after wave, I climbed back down into the engine room, before my absence had gone on too long. Martin looked relieved to see that I was back. He was still having difficulty locating his sea legs. I checked the Genny was running ok, as Martin always appeared to concentrate on the main engines and forget about this vital piece of equipment. Without it the ship would loose all electrical power. Martin disappeared up the ladder to take his turn out on deck. I was thinking about storing my new ghetto blaster down here, under the workbench. Maybe we could try it out tomorrow, see if we could crank the volume up high enough above the rattle and thump of the old engines. In any case, I doubted Trev would be bothered to come looking for it down here. I still didn't trust him to honour the deal we'd made. Once the money I'd just paid him had been squandered, I knew he'd be back for more. I knew, sooner or later, I would have to stand up to him. Some how I had to find a way of appealing to his better nature, or play up to his ego.

I wasn't normally one for inventing strategies to win the influence of my mates and colleagues. It was like being back at the first day of senior school, plunged into an unfamiliar situation. Rumours of a deathly ritual circulated the schoolyard that all the first year boys would be hunted down by the seniors and then be thrown down the embankment at the edge of the playing fields. Some of the more restless boys in my class would even hang around at the top of the banking, hoping to be thrown down it. They felt they had to get it over with, so that they could move on, or even brag about it. The boy who sat next to me at school, in those first few days, was preoccupied with making friends. He was a blond haired lad called Bobby and he'd anxiously quiz me about who I'd made friends with, or how many friends I had. Up until then, it never occurred to me that I had to try hard to make friends, or that there was some sort of ploy to it. I found it easy making friends. I had no favourites; they were just lads to share a laugh with. Maybe that was why I never got into any serious scraps. It helped being able to think on my feet.

I got a shudder down my spine as the picture of my last, near death experience flashed before my eyes. Standing at the back of Jean Casson's car, with his luger pistol pointing at my back, I was glad to have my friends with me at that precise moment in time. If we'd not come up with a diversion tactic, that morning at the Col de la Celeste, I think Jean would have shot all three of us, one by one. There again, I was forgetting that clever and brave intervention by Gingernut. Lucky for us he turned up when he did. He was the unintentional hero that day.

When Martin returned he had a scrumptious looking salad sandwich in his hand.

"I'm not hungry," he said. "Magenta wanted you to have this."

"Cheers, nice one." We sat down, side by side on the tool chest and watched the mesmerising motion of the exposed engine parts: the perpendicular movement of long metal rods, a mesh of rotating cogs, the constant bleeding of oil running down into the vast open sump and the endless thump, thump, thump of the pistons. An occasional spray of salty water blew in through the open portholes. Their cool splashes were a relief from the blue mists of oily heat, inside the engine room.

I asked Martin how he was enjoying being at sea. I thought that if he was going to make a career as a marine engineer, he would have to get used to the ship rolling from side to side. He pulled a packet from his breast pocket.

"I've just took some of these," he said, "sea sickness tablets, Magenta let me have them." He took a sip of water and asked, "How come you're not feeling rough?"

"No idea really. Maybe it's down to the fact I've got wide feet. I've always had good balance. My dad used to say when I was growing up, if my feet got any bigger I would have to start paying ground rent."

After a few more turns at snakes and ladders, taking turns to stand on the poop deck, the signal came through on the telegraph to tell us we were nearing our destination - Half Speed ahead.

Captain Al popped down to forewarn us about our mooring at Ajaccio. "We'll be going in stern to and it's quite a tight, compact marina. There's not a lot a lot of room for manoeuvre, so you're both going to have to be as slick as you can on the telegraph. I'll send you down the slow ahead signal when we're getting close. Keep an eye on the telegraph from then on and we should be fine.

Ten minutes later came the signals to drop down the throttle speeds and stop engines. We could feel the ship starting to turn in. We heard the anchor chain, rattling free from the lockers beneath the fore deck and whizzing out of the hawsehole. The Liberty Angel turned slowly through one hundred and eighty degrees, on her rudder - Slow Astern.

We could see, through the open portholes, the different shapes and sizes of masts from other yachts pass closely by - Stop Engines.

We both looked up at the telegraph dials above our heads and waited for the slow ahead signal. We hardly felt to be moving at all. We could hear Gareth's voice through the porthole. He was shouting back at an angry voice that we didn't recognise. Then came a sudden ring from the telegraph, slow ahead on my engine only. I had my hand on the reverse wheel ready and cranked it anti- clockwise with the throttle position set on idle. Fifteen seconds later - Stop Engines.

"I think we're in," confirmed Martin. Then, thirty seconds later - Finish With Engines. "That's it," he said with a broad smile on his face. We both climbed out onto the poop deck to get a look at our mooring. We were shocked to see how close we were to the yacht in the next berth. There was only a fender width between us.

Gareth stuck his head out of the galley, laughing as usual.

"What was all that shouting about?"

"Sounded like you was having a barney with someone?" Martin added.

"Nah, it was diddly squat. The geezer in the next berth got all panicky when he saw us approaching. He was flapping his arms, saying, "There isn't room, find another berth," mocked Gareth, imitating the geezer's startled look. "Then he started fretting about whether we had any stabilisers below the waterline, sticking out on the side of the hull. Don't think it helped to calm him when I shouted back "I think they've both been knocked off already." He chuckled. "Mind you it was a brilliant piece of piloting by Al, straight in, in one go again.

The old whinge-bag next to us still wasn't happy. We heard him complaining to Al about Gareth's attitude and how Al had laid our anchor chain over the top of his. Al harpooned his last comment, with the reply that we'd be leaving tomorrow and that he seen bigger tin baths than the yacht he was sitting in. That was the last we heard from him.

No sooner had the gangplank been lowered onto the cobbled quayside, than there was Marsha, tiptoeing her way across it, wearing a shiny, sequinned frock, her stilettos dangling from her right hand and a matching gold clutch bag in her left.

"Are you coming Don? The stores will be closing in an hour." Don plodded after her. At least he had the good sense to wear yachty shoes, shame about the white Stetson.

"Wait up, Marsha honey."

"Wait up Marsha," mimicked Gareth, "the poor basket."

We were moored up at the very end section of the ancient harbour wall, which jetted out at an obtuse angle, (I knew learning algebra at school would come in handy one day) from the main western arm of the harbour. In front of us, set towards the centre of the busy, little marina, were around half a dozen long, wooden jetties with smaller craft tied to them. There were, at least a couple of hundred of them, mainly single man yachts and speed boats, of varying length and girth. I followed the wall around the harbour wall to the open quayside where the local fishermen were landing their catch of the day. Behind the stacks of wooden crates, all covered with crushed ice, the promenade was lined with palm trees. The exotic look was strengthened further by a line of historic, five-storied buildings, with hundreds of sun bleached, painted, wooden shutters and a crown of terracotta clay roof tiles, row after row, haphazardly laying a gentle line towards the dome of the basilica, which stood at the top of the sloping hillside - just a footnote to the majestic, rugged mountains in the distance. This wonderful old port had great character. It was no surprise to learn that it was the birthplace of Emperor Napoléon.

Around seven-thirty p.m., all the crew, with the exception of Al and Magenta, were given permission to go ashore. As we walked past our silent neighbours, just before we joined the main arm of the western harbour wall, I recognised the strange looking boat from two days ago when we'd been sheltering from the storm in that barren cove.

As we drew level with the mysterious, dark grey, streamlined hull, a head popped up from a hatch on the aft deck and began speaking to us in English. At the stern, the pale blue and white stripes of the national flag of Greece hung limply and came to rest above the faded, rubbed out lettering of the boat's name - it was barely decipherable - Alios.

"Did you guys just come in with that classic old Thorneycroft vessel?"

"Yer, that's right mate," agreed Trev, stepping forward from our group and sticking his chest out, taking charge as normal. "Don't recognise yours though, but she looks like she's built for speed."

The head belonged to a tattooed English guy, called Pete Wilkinson, from Lincolnshire. The rest of our group stood fidgeting, looking anxious to get moving into town and, sensing Trev's mundane curiosity for all things nautical, they decided to push off. "Leave you to it Trev," announced Gareth, with a hint of sarcasm in his voice.

For some unknown reason, I was quite curious too. The vessel looked oddly out of place, so I decided to follow Trev, up the steel gangplank, when Pete invited us to step aboard. He led us to a windowless door, halfway down the length of the rounded, reinforced superstructure, which only stood around eight feet above the height of the deck. As I passed along the narrow side deck, I couldn't help noticing around half a dozen or more ragged looking holes that seemed to form a diagonal line from aft to fore. Inside the door, Pete handed us both a cold beer from the fridge.

"What do you guys do then?" he asked purposefully.

"I'm responsible for everybody and everything aboard the Liberty Angel. Have been for the last five years. Mostly Charter work: rich Americans and the like."

"Oh aye, sounds like a cushy number. What's the pay like?"

"A pittance," bemoaned Trev, knocking back his beer to take the bad taste of poverty away.

"What about you Byrney?" asked Pete, but before I could answer, Trev struck first with a few derogatory comments,

"He's just a sprog, still green behind the gills."

"Would you like to see below deck?"

"It'd be rude not to, now we've come this far," said Trev, enthusiastically. I was beginning to wish I'd gone along into town with the others. Being the butt of Trev's jokes wasn't my idea of fun, but I was still curious about what secrets this sinister looking vessel held. Once inside the clinically clean engine room, I began to feel uncomfortable. Down the centre of the floor, side by side, were mounted two, slick looking, monster rocket pods, like remnants from NASA's Cape Canaveral.

"Reverse flow, gas turbine, aero engines," disclosed Pete, "Each producing 4000 horse power and weighing in at three tons a piece."

Trev looked assuredly impressed and walked up and touched the aluminium metal casing of one of the engines.

"Bristol Proteus, right?"

"Correct," said Pete, looking surprised. "And you know this because?"

"Long story mate. But we had a stripped down version of one of these in our classroom in my Royal New Zealand Air Cadet days. Our air force back home used them in Bristol Freighters. Spent many a happy hour having the basics of how they worked, drilled into us in the squadron hut." "Great, would you like a job here Trev?"

"Ha ha, you're kidding right?" replied Trev.

"No, seriously, our engineer has had to leave suddenly." I was dying to know how fast this vessel could go. So, to Trev's annoyance, I interrupted their two-way conversation.

"So, how fast is she?"

Pete turned to face me and raised his eyebrows, "Fifty knots."

"Fifty knots," blustered Trev, "that's insane. What sort of vessel is this? Looks more like a MTB to me."

"That's exactly what she is. Built by Vosper in 1960 for the German Navy and lately of the Greek Navy, until my boss bought her."

"So what exactly is it that you do to warrant travelling at fifty bloody knots, because that happens to be about five knots faster than anything else in The Med?" asked Trev, which in part was going to be my next question too.

"Okay, keep this to yourselves." Pete took a step closer. "We smuggle cigarettes. Our last trip netted us fifty thousand pounds - split five ways."

I looked at Trev and could almost hear the cogs rattling inside his head. "What the catch? I mean it's bloody illegal, right?" he said.

"Fifteen years inside an Italian, or a Greek prison, if we're caught." This didn't sound all that appealing to me. I wasn't tempted one little bit, having promised Gastin last year, it was the straight and true from now on. There was no way I'd get involved in something like this for all the tea in China, to quote my mum. This kind of caper was far too reckless.

As we walked away back towards the gangplank, I stopped and stared at those peculiar round holes in the steel bulkhead beside the door. I turned and saw Pete standing next to Trev, looking like he had something to confess.

"The Italians got a bit too close for comfort," confirmed Pete. "Machine gun bullets," he said, being a little economical with the truth.

At breakfast in the ships galley, next morning, Captain Al was in good spirits. The Americans were behaving themselves and being less demanding. The bilges in the engine room were the driest he'd seen them in a long time, thanks to Martin and me and the weather report for our trip back to the French mainland coast was looking very promising. There was just one thing missing;

"Has anyone seen my number two this morning?" A few childish giggles followed. "Okay, you infantile lot, I'll rephrase that. Has anyone seen my second in command?" Al surveyed our faces. Come to think of it, I'd not been woken in the middle of the night by Trev, slamming our cabin door and when he wasn't there this morning, I'd just automatically presumed he was up and at it, organising the daily routines.

Al looked directly at me for an answer. "Byrney?"

"No, I've not seen him since last night."

"Has anyone seen Trev, this morning?"

Silence.

"Well maybe he's slipped ashore on some errand. He knows what time we're sailing. He's got precisely one hour before we leave."

After breakfast I went back down to our cabin to check that Trev hadn't returned whilst the rest of us had been up in the galley together. I stood next to the hatch on the fore deck and just before I climbed down the ladder I looked further down the harbour wall to my left. Then I noticed the empty berth space where the cigarette boat had been moored last night. 'He can't have', I thought. I was beginning to beam from ear to ear, putting two and two together. 'So old Trev's been hooked.'

Five minutes before sailing, I climbed up to the top deck to find Al studying a chart laid out on the narrow table in the wheelhouse. I gave him the news about Trev: that I was ninety-nine per cent certain I knew exactly where he was at this precise moment: on his way to Italy aboard the MTB.

Al's reply was very unexpected too. "Do you know what Byrney? I think we'll manage just as well without him."

Well, I wasn't going to miss him, that was for sure.

Chapter Four

Rosie's Bar

Prior to setting sail last week with 'Les Amercain's', Magenta had parked the team minibus in the port car park, in its usual spot at Cap-d'Ail. For the first time, I was stood close enough to the old Commer camper to see that, even though it was only seven years old, it had had a hard life. Over the years, the Mediterranean sun had bleached the blue paintwork into a fade to grey. I'd seen Magenta and Fionn jump in it regularly, for the weekly grocery run, back to the Carrefour Supermarché in Nice. They always appeared to be having a laugh when they returned, bouncing back down the quayside, with overflowing shopping bags visible through the sliding side windows.

Surprisingly the engine started first turn of the key, although the noise was alarming. The engine, hidden beneath an ill-fitting, black, plastic dome cover, was perched between the two front seats. Conversation was almost on the same level as down in the engine room, but we made a go of it, which was more than could be said of Magenta's attempts at pointing the bus in the right direction, as she fought with the stubborn steering wheel. I could appreciate how cumbersome the right hand steering position must be to drive, and to think that some poor unfortunate sod had driven it all the way out here from South Wales sometime before November 1970 - which was when the current tax disc had expired, nearly seven years ago.

It had been a fraught morning so far and I was glad to get away from the Liberty Angel for a few hours. Also it was a perfect opportunity to get to know more about the 'Queen of Cool' herself. I began by asking her how she came to be here, in this particular part of the world. She was happy to talk a little about her past, provided I didn't interrupt her with any dumb questions. She'd first fallen in love with the Cote d'Azur upon seeing the film 'To Catch A Thief'. She loved the glamour and glitz. As a young student she'd studied fashion and design, but checked out of college because her career was heading nowhere. On an impulse, she jumped on a coach from London to Marseille, then across the French Riviera to Cannes, for the annual film festival, hanging out on the Promenade de la Croisettes and the fashionable resorts of Saint Tropez and Juan les Pins. She was hoping to be one of the lucky faces in the crowd, pulled from obscurity and into the spotlight - the right place at the right time. That was two years ago; it hadn't worked out for her.

I felt like saying that with her sultry looks she shouldn't give up, that it would happen for her one day. But I was conscious of not bugging her with my questions. As we drove along the narrow, bumpy coast road she occasionally removed her gaze from the way ahead and turned her head to face me. Probably, she was checking I was still listening. She continued to explain how she became interested in cooking at an early age. She'd spent a lot of time with her aunt during the summer holidays.

Her aunt lived in the Cornish seaside resort of Newquay and she was a devout follower of Elizabeth David: the lady who, with her partner, had sailed the length and breadth of the Mediterranean before the war. Magenta glanced at me for some sign of recognition; I smiled blankly.

"She'd discovered a world of wonderfully delicious cuisine, of oils, spices and fresh herbs," continued Magenta. "My aunt had all Elizabeth David's cookery books and she taught me how to cook, how to make mouth watering salad dressings and to use my nose as well as my taste buds. So with all this knowledge handed down to me, it seemed a shame to waste it. So that's how I ended up in this part of the world, as you say."

I hadn't much of a clue about these things, but it sounded very impressive. Then she asked me about whether Fionn and me were an item, since we'd arrived here at roughly the same time.

I told her about how we'd worked together at the Friary in Crowston. Then the short version about how we'd come to France last autumn and my quest to deliver Eve's ashes to her husband's grave on the Col du Monde.

"Someone was going to kill you!" she shouted out loud. "Christ Byrney, you should be more careful at your age."

"When we get to Hotel Les Moulins," I replied, "I'll introduce you to Eve's brother-in-law. He said the same thing to me too."

When we screeched to a halt on Rue Lazarette, Henri and Juliette were both very pleased to see me. They said Fionn was staying with Patrice at his studio. She was too ashamed to face them and too afraid to become embroiled in any further altercations working at their hotel. I introduced them to Magenta, but knowing we only had a limited amount of time to collect Fionn and bring her back on board. We bade them farewell, apologising for our flying visit. As I was leaving, Juliette said, "please come back again and stay with us one evening. We haven't thanked you properly yet for what you did for Eve.

I led Magenta around the corner, rattled the door at 'Hard Hat Graphiques' and stepped inside. Fionn looked at us without saying a word and I immediately saw how troubled she looked. It was not like her to hold herself back. Normally she'd be leaping through the air in my direction. Patrice looked relieved when he learnt we'd come to collect Fionn. We were expecting to see her bags out, packed and ready to go. But she had no intention of leaving.

"How can I come back with this horrible thing hanging over me. I'm staying right here until I can clear my name."

"Look Fi, no one believes you stole Marsha's jewels, not for one minute. Come on; come back with us. Everyone is really looking forward to seeing you again."

It was Magenta's turn to try and talk sense to Fionn. I thought it best not to mention all the trouble that met us on the quayside when we had moored up in Cannes, earlier this morning. Marsha had gone overboard with her calls for justice regarding her missing jewels. Whilst we'd been in Ajaccio she'd called ahead to the Port Police in Cannes, The Gendarmes and even the Douane customs people were summoned to intercept us on our arrival.

"All that's missing is bloody Interpol," observed Gareth as the hoards of uniformed offices searched the Liberty Angel and took statements from everyone, including the guests. Even poor old hen-pecked Don was quizzed.

Of course they all left empty handed, promising to follow up the next day. The Port Police were given the task of announcing a reward of two thousand dollars for any information leading to the jewels being found. None of the crew was convinced. It still seemed favourite to us that this was an insurance set up, especially as Marsha seemed well versed with the procedure of obtaining an investigation case number. Whether any of the authorities on board were possibly thinking along the same lines, or whether it was simply procedural practice, was hard to tell. But Marsha responded angrily at being asked to maintain her whereabouts to the Police.

"That won't be necessary," she confirmed. "Don and I will be staying at the Carlton, room 505, for the next seven days. Our friends Roger, Bill and Vivienne will be staying in adjacent rooms." Then turning to Al for one last time before she left, she added, "I'm desperate for some real luxury. If you think leaving a piece of candy on my pillow qualifies, then you're dumber than you look. I've seen better equipped yachts on The Lake in Central Park."

The crew gave her a round of applause as she left, not realising the applause was directed at her going, rather than because they agreed with her. We watched all the uniformed, French officers file out along the busy quayside.

"Blimey," commented Gareth. "If anyone sees that lot leaving, we'll be known as the Convict Ship."

Magenta spilt the beans to Fionn, giving her the gist of what had occurred just before we picked her up in Nice.

"Right," she said, grabbing her bags and kissing Patrice on both cheeks. "Take me to the Carlton."

I shrugged my shoulders at Patrice and smiled, "désolé mon ami, à bientôt."

Patrice handed two envelopes, addressed to me, saying "See you soon."

I quickly glanced at the postage stamps, then folded the envelopes in half and placed them inside my back pocket. It would have been great to have caught up with Patrice in more detail, but Fionn was already parked in the front passenger seat of Magenta's mini bus. We drove the forty kilometres back to Cannes in a solidified silence from Fionn. We tried cajoling her with our experiences over the past seven days, but our tales were water off a duck's back. Fionn only spoke to insist on confronting Marsha first before she had any intention of stepping across the gangplank again onto the Liberty Angel.

Magenta dropped us right outside the Carlton Hotel entrance, saying she'd drive once around the block. "Don't be long," she added.

I'd never seen a more impressive looking building in all my life. We fumbled our way through the giant revolving door. I'd been nervous before we entered, but as soon as we were inside the foyer, I began to feel incredibly uncomfortable at the five-star grandeur. It isn't a hotel, I thought, it's a palace. Several huge, marble columns stretched right up to the golden, decorated ceiling panels, each one suspending a heavy chandelier, dripping with diamonds. I tried to pull Fionn back outside.

"Come on Fi, we're not meant to be here." But she broke free and marched straight across to the concierge desk. The wooden panelled desk was dressed with half a dozen, matching, shaded table lamps. No expense spared. The opulent atmosphere was personified in the suspicious look, which greeted us from the behind the counter.

Fionn spoke in French to the immaculate, uniformed man, demanding to speak to the American couple, Marsha and Don in room 505.

"You mean Madame and Monsieur McGruder," replied the concierge in English.

"Yes, that's them," seared Fionn, fighting to keep her composure.

"Who shall I say is calling?" He picked up the desk telephone and let it ring for thirty seconds. "I'm sorry there doesn't appear to be anyone at home."

"Well I'm not leaving until I speak to someone. Try Roger what's his name in the next room."

I watched the concierge dial 506 and within a few seconds a voice answered. The concierge explained he had a mademoiselle…" he turned to Fionn. Then he passed the details on to the voice at the other end of the line.

Within a minute, I recognised the slim, slightly hunched frame of Roger Martin as he emerged from the lift. Fionn spotted him at the same moment and demanded to speak to Marsha. Roger apologised on her behalf, saying she was in town and wouldn't be returning until much later.

"Well you can inform Mrs Toffee Nose McGruder that I've spoken to the Police myself this morning and told them everything I know, that it's my belief she stole the jewels herself. Perhaps you'll be kind enough to pass that message on." Fionn's voice was getting louder by the word. She'd stopped at least a dozen, well heeled, passing guests in their tracks, who were now standing, staring at us. A second concierge had walked around the front of the counter and was heading straight for us. I could see he intended on removing us.

"Come on Fi, let's go before we get arrested."

"Watch out for Marsha McGruder," she yelled as we turned away. "That woman is a compulsive liar."

We hurried back out onto the promenade. "It's not what I was hoping for, but at least I feel better for saying it," Fionn grumbled.

Magenta was waiting on the opposite side of the boulevard, in our getaway vehicle - the old Commer. She was sat behind the wheel, with the engine running as we dashed inside. Fionn jumped into the front seat, leaving me to slide back the side door for myself.

"Well done Fionn, for standing up to them," said Magenta. "No one on board has a good word to say about her, especially after the inquisition we've been put through this morning."

"Yer let's get back on board and we can all forget about it," I said. I was looking forward to putting a little distance between us and the Carlton Hotel. After a while we all began to laugh about Fionn's showdown. Now that it was all over, I could see the funny side - poor Roger.

Later that evening, Fionn came down to my cabin, to sound me out about a few of her theories. She still wasn't letting go. We ruled Trev out. It was probably just a coincidence that he'd done a runner before Marsha started with her accusations.

"So if you don't think any of the crew stole the jewels - it has to be one of them."

"My money is going on Marsha," declared Fionn.

There wasn't much else to say about who'd taken them, or if anyone would actually be able to claim a reward for finding them. Fionn began to tell me more about her week in Nice. She was offered her old room at Les Moulins, but it was obvious Jean-Paul was being very tiresome, with his attempts to rekindle their romance.

"It was embarrassing actually," said Fionn. "Patrice had to have a word with his friend and spelt it out in language Jean-Paul understood - Foutez-elle la paix ok - Back off.

After Fionn had left and said goodnight, I lifted my pillow and removed the two letters that had been waiting for me at Patrice's. I recognised Anna's handwriting and the US Airmail postage stamp was a bit of a giveaway. The other letter was more intriguing with its 'Correos Aero De Bolivia' blue and white stamp - it had to be from Gastin de Bourges.

I opened the one from Anna first. As I read the first two opening sentences I became sort of light headed and my hand began to shake. Her words had begun to drill down inside me and I was finding it difficult to focus on them. There wasn't the slightest hint of any compassion. It was as if our love had never existed at all and now - it was over between us. She had found someone new. His name is Jim. The rest of the letter sounded like blah, blah, blah. I was shocked just how much it got to me. It was true I hadn't heard from her since our tearful parting at Toulouse Matabiau Station and I had expected her to forget about me, once she settled back into college life; but still, she was always in my thoughts. I was so proud of her. I had so much respect for her. When I put down the letter, it left me feeling totally helpless.

The letter from Gastin failed to cheer my mood. He wrote about the difficulties and the obstacles he was facing. The situation also sounded quite dangerous. 'The man I am chasing,' he wrote, ' is very well protected, by the most powerful authority here. The regime in Bolivia is very tyrannical, just like the bad old days in France. It's almost as if the Nazi's still hold the whip in their hands. People are disappearing without trace all the time. Anyone who speaks out against President Suarez is taken away and tortured, or worse. Students, trade unionists, communists and even Jews are constantly in danger. The atmosphere is so repressive. It's as if the man I'm chasing is working his influence behind the scenes.' Gastin asked what I was doing, if I was still in Nice? Had I heard from Anna?

I was genuinely worried for Gastin. But he was a born survivor and he knew when to ask for help. I promised myself to reply to his letter, although he mentioned he might have to move across the border to Argentina. He mentioned a town called San Carlos de Bariloche, in the Andes Mountains, which was, supposedly, a haven for ex-Nazis and war criminals. He'd be much more at home there, with his knowledge of conquering that type of terrain. He was one determined hunter and I was totally in awe of him.

****

For once, the sun was also shining at exactly the same time in West Lancashire, though not exactly the same time, as the clocks in the UK were still one hour behind the rest of the Continent, including the south of France. The month of May was normally a wet month, so it made a change to get the hood rolled back and blow away a few cobwebs. The trees were turning into full grown, thickness and the adult birds were busy working in shifts to keep their hungry young fed and watered.

At precisely one-thirty p.m there was a screech of rubber rounding the corner at the entrance of Churchtown Close. A flashy sports car drove down the centre of the quiet cul-de-sac and drew onto the tarmac drive, coming to a halt a foot away from the freshly painted pair of green, garage doors.

A tall figure alighted, grabbed his case from the rear seat, folded his double-breasted sports jacket over his arm, and picked up the bunch of flowers too. He walked over to the front door, passing and smiling at the 'Sold' sign, hanging from the board at the edge of the garden. He rang the bell and waited, feeling an immense sensation of self-satisfaction. He heard the delicate pitter-patter of tiny elephant feet descending the stairs and within seconds the door was yanked open. Sandra Atkinson pulled down the hem of her mini-skirt and looked up with surprise.

"Oh, it's you. What are you ringing the bell for?" Lofty held out the bunch of flowers which immediately softened Sandra's heart. "Argh, welcome home love."

Lofty stepped forward pressing himself against her and squeezing her bum from behind.

"Come inside, quick. You'll have all the neighbours talking again."

Lofty put down his case and followed her into the familiar surroundings of the homely lounge.

"I've been doing some thinking, while you've been away all week." She said, teasingly.

Lofty spied all the holiday brochures scattered on the onyx marble top coffee table. "I've got something for you too." He smiled and retrieved a rolled up piece of imitation parchment from his jacket pocket. He slid the ribbon along to the end and unfolded it slowly. "Look at that - Bryn Davis M.B.E."

"You daft bugger. What does it say really?"

"Bryn Davis M.B.E," repeated Lofty. "I've always wanted one"

"Let me see." Sandra stared at the red wax seal in the name of 'Wilshaws Brewery'. "Ooh, look at that, Bryn Davis, Master Brewer, England." She looked proudly at Lofty and continued reading aloud. "This is to certify that the above candidate has successfully completed a pub master's diploma."

"Not bad for a week's work, hey love? So what are all these colourful brochures about: Cosmos, Enterprise, Thomas Cook Cruises..." he frowned.

"Don't worry love. I know we can't run to a fancy cruise, but how about a couple of weeks somewhere warm before we get stuck into our new venture?

"P.T.K.O." he announced as he slumped down into the worn out sofa - Put The Kettle On.

It's true, he thought, they had had a stressful couple of months. Atkinson CID, Sandra's estranged husband had insisted on slinging them out on their arses, when he sneakily put the family home up for sale. But Sandra and Lofty were always one step ahead of him. They both knew him too well to let him get away with it. 'S.T.Y' Lofty reminded himself - Smarter Than You. There was no way Atkinson was going to have it all his own way. They were staying put, until the house sale went through via the correct channels. Besides, neither of them trusted him. He wasn't going to cheat Sandra out of her half share of eighteen thousand pounds. With the money coming to her and Lofty's cash from his insurance claim, when his flat had been demolished in the mysterious arson attack, they had already agreed to take on the tenancy agreement at the Bull's Head Inn at Churchtown village.

They had grand plans for the old, 'Mock Tudor' fronted ale-house. They'd discussed starting up a Tote Betting Club, with profits going towards annual trips to the seaside at Southport - family outings for the regulars. By pooling their bets together on horse racing, they would have a greater chance of winning. And now that Lofty had gained the necessary qualifications on running a pub, together with Sandra's barmaid experience, they both felt they couldn't lose. As soon as spring-time had arrived, their semi-detached house in the secluded cul-de-sac sold, surprisingly quickly. The housing market was going through a mini boom period, after the slumps it had suffered during the energy crisis of the early and mid nineteen-seventies. This new boom in housing confidence had been partly fuelled too, by the growing morale of the nation, in the wake of Queen Elizabeth II's silver jubilee celebrations. Her perambulations across her kingdom filled the news bulletins on a daily basis. Ordinary people flocked to the streets, in their thousands, to greet their smiling and gracious monarch. The royal entourage would even be passing close by on June 20th, when she planned to visit Lancaster and Preston. It was a great time to be a patriot, thought Lofty. 'I shall have to polish my medals.'

They sat happily together, flicking through the brochures, hoping for inspiration. "Is there somewhere special you've always wanted to go?" asked Lofty, feeling mesmerised by all the choices available to them.

"Well," paused Sandra. "I've always wanted to go to the casino at Monte Carlo, in a posh frock."

"That's not such a bad idea. If we go either side of Spring Bank Holiday, we can catch the Monaco Grand Prix at the same time."

Sandra threw her arms around Lofty's neck, planting a kiss on the side of his chin and spilling his cup of tea over his trousers.

"That settles it," said Lofty, standing up and revealing a damp patch, like he'd just peed his pants. "M.C.C here we come."

****

The schedule for Liberty Angel, after a couple of nights moored in our old berth at Cap d'Ail, was to return to Monte Carlo for the rest of the week. Our next charter came from the prestigious American company, Champion - famous for their spark plugs. The five day charter would see us permanently based in Monte Carlo, as our vessel had been hired solely to be used as a venue for hospitality, during the forth coming, Monaco Grand Prix.

65

I volunteered to help out with waiting on, as Trev's sudden departure had left us a man down in that department. Gareth and Magenta were in charge of making all the decisions regarding refreshments and seating.

After taking up our temporary berth on the Quai l'Hirondelle, in Monte Carlo harbour, Al was called back to South Wales, to explain the nature of the Police investigations in connection to the missing jewels which had now reached head office, back in the UK. I think Al was still working on the theory it was an insurance racket.

When the two American marketing directors arrived on board, they handed out white t-shirts to all of us. The front was emblazened with the iconic Champion logo. And there was also a matching pair of white overalls for the engineer. I really fancied them for myself, but was happy for Martin to take them.

Each morning, the view from the fore deck began to grow and change as the technicians and contractors undertook the mammoth task, of converting the sea front into a modern race circuit. First, miles of cabling was laid for the public address system. Seven foot tall, wire mesh fencing drew a line around the town. From our mooring, looking towards the race-track, we were plumb between the exit of the tunnel and the Port Chicane. It would be a great vantage point to view the race. Just a few paces further down the sea front, scaffolders were busy, piecing together the make shift grandstand. It looked to me like a giant Meccano set.

Most of the hospitality we provided comprised of large, cold buffets, which normally took place in the afternoon, or early evening. It was very exciting to be so closely involved with such a big, corporate event. I was keeping my fingers crossed I would get a chance to meet the current Formula One world champion, James Hunt.

As we were handily placed below the centre of Monte Carlo, it was only a twenty minutes walk up to Casino Square. Not that I was attracted to going there. Besides we were never dressed for it. Instead, we'd stop off half way up the hill and spend the night in Rosie's Bar. It hadn't changed from last

October, when we'd called in for a beer, on our way to play Craps at the casino with Patrice and Jean-Paul.

Behind the bar, I was pleased to see Rosie again, serving drinks and chatting up the male customers. She was still wearing her long, white hair tied up in a sixties beehive and although she only spoke a smidge of English, I really liked her. She seemed unflappable and performed her hostessness with a casual ease. She obviously knew every square inch of the place. There were no tables outside, as the pavement was quite narrow and inside too, tended to be standing room only. There was always a gang of locals, crowded around the pinball machine, and the chiming of the bells and buffers added to the noisy atmosphere. Music came from a radio that sat on a shelf behind the bar, tuned into old, French crooning, which possibly only Rosie heard as she ambled back and forth.

It was good to see Fionn back to her old self again. She'd really impressed me, the way she'd bounced back from the Marsha jewel affair. Fionn and Magenta were getting pretty close these days. Their friendship had now blossomed into them dressing alike. Because they shared a cabin together, they were most likely sharing each other's clothes too. Tonight they were both wearing cheese-cloth blouses which had an elasticated band at the top that was worn with both shoulders bare. They both had a version of flared, blue denim jeans. Fionn's pockets, at the back, had broad red, white and blue stitching around them, kind of cute, I thought.

The fashionable drink of the moment was seize soixante quatre - sixteen sixty-four beer, drank straight from the bottle. As it was grand prix week, there were a much greater number of visitors and foreigners frequenting the town, lots of British of course, all here to cheer on their champion. As more and more people piled in, we were pushed further away from the bar. Gareth was entertaining us with his trick with beer mats. He was pretending to throw them and when we all looked back at him, he'd stuck a beer mat to the bridge of his nose, as if he'd been impaled.

At the other end of the packed room, I suddenly caught a flash of something, which alarmed me. It was only a fleeting glimpse of someone moving quickly between the gaps in the crowd. As the unnerving moment subsided, I was beginning to doubt my own eyes. Had I just seen a tall man with a thick thatch of ginger hair? I shifted from side to side and stared in the same direction, but there was no such person. Just a middle aged woman, with dyed blond hair, looking over dressed for the occasion.

The empty, blue bottles of beer were fanning out around our table. The atmosphere was reaching deafening proportions and yet more people kept filing in and out. After four bottles of beer, I had to visit the little hommes room. Closing the door behind me, revealed a single pissoir and the usual trap door with just a single dark hole in the floor and a couple of raised, rectangular pads to line your-self up by. With the door closed the noise from the bar was barely audible. As I turned around to leave, there, stood behind me and blocking my exit was the one man I thought I'd never clap eyes on again - Gingernut.

He looked like he was doing alright for himself in his white blazer and black, dickie bow tie, very 007. He was obviously out to impress.

"I thought it was you," he said. "I think we need to have a little chat." He looked serious, but as yet to my relief, unthreatening.

"What about?"

"That money you stole from the Post Office at Crowston for starters," he growled.

I was starting to panic. For one thing he had me cornered. Surely he must know that the money has gone. I was thinking hard and fast about what I was going to say to him so that I could somehow make my escape. "I'm glad your wounds have healed okay," I said sincerely.

Just then the toilet door was forced open and Gareth walked in. "Here you are - it's your round. No good trying to hide." Before he'd finished talking, I made a dash to join him in the open doorway. Gareth headed back into the bar. As I quickly stepped out to join him, Gingernut grabbed hold of my left arm. He had a strong grip. His spade of a hand almost wrapped itself fully around my bicep.

"Meet me in here, tomorrow at noon, alone."
I nodded in agreement - anything just to get out of there.

Rosie closed the bar at exactly ten-thirty p.m. At her age, I didn't blame her. The lights behind the bar were switched off and a towel hung limply over the single, electric pump for the beer tap. She stood beside the open door encouraging us all to leave. "Allons sie. On y va. Let's go. Tout le monde."
The contre-temps in the gents toilet earlier had put a real dampener on the whole evening. But my shipmates were, unknowingly, not about to let me feel sorry for myself. As we walked back down the pavement towards the marina, we couldn't stop ourselves from breaking out into a run. The street was almost empty, save for a few odd cars, which were making their way up to the square. As we ran down the hill, I heard laughter and giggling breaking out behind me. When I glanced around to see what the fun was about. I couldn't believe my eyes. Magenta's elasticated cheese-cloth top had accidentally slipped down to her waist and she was trying to pull it back over her bare boobs as she carried on running. She never stopped laughing. She didn't care. I was the only one to see what had happened. Even Fionn who was running beside her hadn't noticed. Suddenly, for that moment, everything was alright again in the world.

The following morning, we were all stood in our usual places, around the makeshift table, inside the galley. Thanks to Gingernut turning up here in Monte Carlo, I'd not had a good night's sleep. I was feeling very unnerved by his sudden reappearance. And I was feeling tired and angry too - this was my world, my place to escape to from my past mistakes. What could he possibly want from me now? Whatever it was, I knew somehow I had to face up to him, or I'd be looking over my shoulder for the rest of my life.
I was watching Magenta preparing a continental breakfast for our guests, the Champion Marketing Team. Every once in a while, she would catch me staring at her and smile back at me. We were the only ones present to share the same private joke.

She hadn't attempted to hide her embarrassment about what had happened on the way back to the boat last night. It wasn't that she didn't care. it seemed to me like it was more of a case of whom she chose to show her feelings to. Right now she looked like she knew exactly what I was thinking. Was it that obvious? I could feel my eyes broaden into giving my thoughts away, that I could still picture her running behind me, naked from the naval up. Had it been my trousers that had fallen down instead of her top, I would have had to keep my embarrassment hidden away for a week.

Just then, Gareth appeared from the wheel house, on the top deck.

"I've just had a strange conversation over the radio phone," He said, catching our attention. "Old man Bailey was wanting to know where Al is?" We all looked at one another without replying. Gareth continued, "I told him as far as anyone here knew, he left a couple of days ago and was heading straight back to head office in Barry."

We were all trying to think what could have happened. It was so out of character for Al to disappear like that. Gareth turned to Dozy Dave and asked him exactly what Al had said that morning when he'd left. Dave had been the last one to see him. Dave stood fidgeting, rooted to the spot at being the focus of our combined attention.

"All he said to me was, he was going to get some staples."

"Hello?" winced Gareth in exasperation, "Monte Carlo calling Dave… that just doesn't make any sense." "Well that's what it sounded like to me," he replied timidly.

Fionn stepped in front of me and pinched my arm, prompting me to follow her out onto the poop deck. I could tell there was something on her mind.

"What's up Fi?" I said, out of earshot of the galley.

"Do you think Al could have taken Marsha's jewels?"

Fionn's comments had caught me off guard. I hadn't got as far as putting Al's disappearance together with the stolen jewels.

"I can't see Al doing that," I said. "He's got too much at stake here, too much to lose."

Later that morning, just before noon, I invented a reason to nip ashore - we needed some new bulbs for the bulkhead lamps inside the engine room - So I let Gareth know I was off to the ships' chandlers, at the Rascasse Restaurant end of the harbour. This was the chandler we normally used. We'd renamed it 'Hooligans', for the simple reason that one morning Dave had gone there looking unshaven, dishevelled and slightly worse for wear and the proprietor had said to him in broken English, "you look like a Hooligan."

I used one of the new pedestrian elevators, from the swimming pool complex up to Casino Square and walked back down to Rosie's, aiming to call in at Hooligan's on my way back. I saw the square shouldered figure of Gingernut, sat waiting for me, with his back against the far wall of the bar. He was slowly submerging sugar cubes into his cafe au lait. When I reached his table, without looking up at me he said, "Argh, nice to meet you again. I'd almost given up on you."

"Listen Bryn." (I'd remembered his name from the hospital in St. Jean where he'd been recovering from the gunfight with Jacques Casson) "Listen I haven't much time so I'm just going to tell it how it is, that is, whatever you want from me I don't have anymore." I thought honesty was the best policy and the quicker I said what I needed to, the sooner I'd be out of here. The man opposite me didn't show the slightest emotion to what I'd just said. I could spot a holiday maker a mile off and from the casual way he dressed, he looked to me like he wasn't here on business. Apart from his glaringly bright head of ginger hair, he blended into the crowded bar very easily.

"And if you're thinking of blackmailing me, I've got nothing of any value to give you," I added for good measure.

Gingernut smiled at me and with an economy of movement slowly took a sip of his coffee. If he was trying to prolong my agony - it was working. He raised his hand in the air and caught a glimpse of the old woman behind the bar.

"Coffee?" He enquired in my direction.

"I haven't time." I explained nervously.

"N.S.F Byrne, not so fast." He ordered another cafe au lait and readjusted his position in his seat.

"Right, first of all," he said holding out his right spade to shake my hand, "I want to thank you for not pressing charges against me and to apologise for chinning you back home, last year."

I frowned, thinking this conversation must eventually be heading towards some place I wasn't going to enjoy.

"I'm guessing it was also down to you that I was given that bundle of cash too, in the plain brown envelope?" he continued.

The coffee arrived and I was beginning to lower my guard a little. I told Gingernut the whole story: how I'd been cajoled into getting involved in the Post Office raid, how my accomplices had both died and how their separate deaths had affected me. And afterwards, being in sole possession of the cash, I'd tried to make amends and that what was left of it was now in South America. I also mentioned that if it hadn't been for the armed guard outside his hospital ward last year, I was going to confront him to say thank you for saving our lives.

"Then the loot is being put to good use. And that's an end to it," he sighed.

He unfolded the paper napkin and wiped the froth from his top lip. "Look Byrne, I'm not after you. When I saw you last night, quite by chance, I just had to know the rest of the story. I'd invested a lot of time and effort trailing you and trying to puzzle out what that bent cop, Atkinson, was being so sneaky about. I was once a detective too and a damn good one in my opinion."

Sounds lovely, I thought, but I really had to be getting back to work. I didn't want Gareth thinking I was taking advantage of Al's absence. We'd a busy afternoon ahead of us, getting ready for the next on board, hospitality party. But listening to Gingernut's last comment had given me an idea.

"Bryn, how good are you at finding lost jewels?"

My question immediately lit up his eyes with a 'one hundred and fifty watt' illumination. He grinned, unable to resist this kind of a challenge. " What jewels?" He said, "and what's in it for me?"

"A two thousand dollar reward."

Chapter Five

To Catch A Thief

Captain Al turned up first thing the next morning, Saturday, the day of the Formula One practice sessions. After arriving on the overnight train from Rome, it had taken him an hour to get through all the temporary security gates around the race circuit to gain access to our side of the marina. Lucky for him, he spoke fluent French.

The night before, there had been a massive hospitality party aboard our vessel. All the formula one teams had been invited: drivers, managers, head mechanics and other team officials. I was excitedly involved all evening, carrying various trays of drinks around the lounge, aft deck and top deck. Gareth and Magenta had bought in dozens of bottles of Moët and Chandon, champagne as requested by our hosts to impress their clientele. As it turned out, nearly all the drivers only drank soft drinks, nearly all, except the English hero, James Hunt. I was hoping to get near him and wish him luck. Unfortunately, our champion hosts had already warned us not to ask for any autographs, or to take any pictures. There was just one photographer present, and he was under the strict supervision of our marketing directors, who were taking sole ownership for all photographic opportunities. Well, I guess they were paying for the privilege.

By nine-thirty p.m. the party guests had all but left. No doubt they had more pressing things on their minds. When the organisers of the party had retired to their cabins for the night, we all finished off clearing up. The galley was covered with half empty bottles of champagne. We passed them around but there were still far too many left to consume and it seemed such an extravagant waste to pour them down the sink. Magenta suggested we line them up out of sight, on the fore deck and place tea-spoons upside down in the open bottles. This would prevent flies from landing inside them.

When we woke the next morning, it was a strange sight to see them all, clinking away to the rhythm of the sea. We emptied a few more bottles at breakfast by mixing them with orange juice. Consequently, by the time Al showed up he was chuffed to see us all together, but slightly puzzled by the impromptu, cheery round of applause we gave him. The mystery of Al's whereabouts for the past four days soon became clear to us. He hadn't stolen the jewels as Fionn had half suspected, no, but dozy Dave had almost been right. Al had not gone to buy some staples - he'd been in Naples - Naples Poggioreale Prison to be exact.

When Al had visited the Port Office to register our arrival in Monte Carlo earlier this week, there was a telegram waiting for him from New Zealand Trev. He'd been arrested aboard the Alios, attempting to smuggle several hundred cases of contraband cigarettes.

"It's a god awful place he's landed himself in," explained Al. "The conditions are atrocious. On top of that there are people locked up there who've been waiting to go to trial for months. Apparently the Italian judicial system is notoriously slow, held up by a huge backlog of cases." Al paused to look around at our shocked faces. "His best chance of getting out would be to try and escape," he said dryly. "I've heard, lots do, The old fashioned way, sawing through the bars. When I was allowed to see Trev, I had to line up with all the other visitors in this long room, us lot on one side of the metal bars and all the prisoners lined up on the other. As you can imagine, Trev was not in the best of spirits. Some of the other inmates I saw next to him looked like mass murderers."

We stood in silence as Al continued to tell us snippets of his experiences, trying to picture what it must be like for Trev, a total stranger in a foreign, dirty jail, with little hope of rescue. It was true he'd been a nuisance and a bully to me and to some of the other crew, Dave and Magenta in particular. Now it seemed the shoe was on the other foot, yet I still couldn't help feeling sorry for him.

When I bumped into Al later, he confided in me that he'd held the worse news back from the girls during breakfast.

"It was common knowledge at the prison that certain inmates were taken down to Room Zero, to be tortured into making a confession. Even the prison governor was said to be on the Mafia payroll. What a place. It reeked of sweat and shit. Trev begged me to persuade Liberty Yachts to help pay for his release. But when I spoke to old man Bailey later, from my hotel room in Naples, he'd washed his hands of him - it was bad publicity for the company and besides Trevor had already walked out on us. No, he was more concerned about who this Gareth North-Lewis character was, whom I'd left in charge? He was worried that someone with a double barrel sounding surname must be spying for the Lloyds Register, or worse the shipping insurers."

"But Trev had worked for Liberty Yachts for the last five years." I couldn't believe that after all he'd put me through, I was still trying to defend Trev. "Surely that counts for something?"

"It's like I said to you before, Byrney. There's no sentiment in business. And as for loyalty, all you're entitled to is a wage packet at the end of the week, and after that there's nothing more to be owed."

It all seemed wrong to me. I also thought that if you gave respect to your elders and betters, you could count on them to do the same in reverse. According to Al I was making the classic mistake of letting my personal issues cloud my judgement.

"So that's it then, he's just going to be left there to rot?"

"Perhaps," said Al philosophically. "But after I'd spoken to Harry Bailey, I did eventually manage to get through to Trev's parents in New Zealand. Whilst I was there I gave them the name of a local solicitor. It's down to them to sort it out now."

Normally the weekends were our own and free to spend them doing whatever we liked. And although the Champion

Marketing people were staying on board until after the race on Sunday afternoon, Al had given most of us permission to go ashore as all our scheduled hospitality events were now completely done.

The race practise sessions were roaring away. First the high-pitched revving of the Formula Three cars came echoing out of the tunnel beneath the Loews Hotel. Then, one hour later, came the distinctive, deeper sounding grunt of the Formula One engines. I'd cadged hold of Fionn's little automatic camera and had bought a couple of 110mm film cassettes earlier in the week. I planned to watch the race at the Port Chicane, which was adjacent to the end of our quayside and directly accessible from our berth. I thought at this point of the racetrack the cars would be going slow enough to capture them on my borrowed camera. However, this was proving quite difficult to judge. I had a couple of practices and worked out my timing for getting a full car in the frame. All I had to do then was to wait for the ninety seconds or so, for the cars to come round again on the next lap, having taking a mental note of the car in front of my target.

Until the practise sessions were done for the day, it was impossible to cross the circuit to get up into the centre of town. I kept checking my watch. I'd made arrangements to rendez-vous with Gingernut at Rosie's at precisely three p.m, not that it was as simple as Gingernut had made it out to be. "Trust your old Uncle Bryn, Byrney, the simple plans are always the best.'

It was all very simple to him as he was already in the company of his girlfriend. I had to produce someone who could pass for my wife. Then, the four of us were going to waltz into the Carlton Hotel in Cannes, all casual-like and figure out how to get up to Room 505 to find the missing jewels.

It had been easier to persuade Magenta to go along with our little scheme than I first thought. Easier, because she was such a big fan of the film 'To Catch A Thief' starring Cary Grant and Grace Kelly, who now lived in the castle on the hill outside our marina. "Small world isn't it?" she said smiling. The Carlton Hotel featured heavily in the famous Nineteen-Fifties film and she longed to spend some time inside, rubbing shoulders with the rich and famous. "It's going to be full of film people. The festival starts next week too."

"What festival?"

"Where have you been, Byrney? Haven't you heard of the Cannes film festival?" I sensed myself blushing uncontrollably as I pretended I already knew that.

The practise sessions ended around two p.m. According to the race announcer over the public address speakers, the British driver John Watson was on pole position and the champagne drinking James Hunt was way down on the fourth row of the grid.

I'd shaken off Martin's attentions of wanting to spend the day with me by saying I was heading back to Nice, to meet up with an old friend. It wasn't entirely a lie, as we would be passing through there on our way to Cannes. I didn't like letting Martin down as he always spent such a lot of time by himself, studying mostly. But I was even more annoyed at myself for getting drawn into helping Gingernut to get his hands on Marsha's jewels.

I grabbed a bottle of beer at the bar and walked over to Bryn's table. He was seated alone, in exactly the same position as two days ago. This time he was dressed to kill. The same white sports jacket as when we first bumped into each other, the same black bow tie, the same James Bondesque look. I was starting to feel uncomfortable already, very conscious of my own appearance in my yachty uniform: white short sleeved shirt and matching trousers with my blue yachty shoes. I wasn't wearing socks and the blue dye from the leather had discoloured my toes. I was praying I wouldn't be asked to take them off at some point.

We exchanged pleasantries and I sat down opposite him, keeping myself out of arms reach.

"So where's your wife?" enquired Gingernut, looking over my shoulder.

"She'll be here in a minute or two," I said, checking my watch for the umpteenth time. "Probably just trying to find somewhere to park the minibus."

Gingernut accepted my answer then scanned around the bar. "Where's you're girlfriend?" I asked.

"Sandra? She's just powdering her nose." Gingernut leaned forward, took a key from his breast pocket and slid it across the table towards me.

"What's this for?" I asked, not really wanting to know. The least I knew about what he had in store the better. In my mind I had a woeful feeling that we were both going to be caught red handed by one of the officious looking concierge staff. I'd already narrowly avoided being collared at the Carlton hotel with Fionn.

"That's the master key to all the bedrooms on the fifth floor at the Carlton," he boasted. "Borrowed it myself this morning from one of the maids trolleys whilst I was on a R.M, recognisance mission."

At that moment a tall, blonde haired, middle aged woman, dressed like one of Pan's People doing a Hawkwind number, strode over and stood next to Bryn. She was wearing a two-piece, silver outfit that appeared to be made from Bacofoil. 'Bloody hell,' I thought, 'let's hope everyone else is going to be in fancy dress at the Carlton. What with 007, silver lady, me in my white outfit and Magenta looking like the queen of cool, we were going to stand out like four clowns at a funeral.'

"Sandra, this is the young man from Lancashire I've been telling you about, meet Byrney." She held out her right hand. I was going to bend down and kiss it. Then, at the last minute, I noticed her long, red, varnished fingernails. Doing my best not to hesitate, I changed my mind and shook it gently instead.

"Pleased to meet you," I lied.

"Here you are love, sit yourself down here," said Bryn, giving up his seat. "Fancy another drink darling?"

"Get me one as well, please Bryn." I said trying not to sound desperate and thinking it was time I dropped his 'Gingernut' label.

Bryn looked at me and sensed I was feeling nervous. "Don't worry about the Carlton, Byrney," He said reassuringly as he walked over to the bar. "All we have to do is blend into the background. P.O.P. Piece of piss."

'Oh, great, is that all' I thought. I stared awkwardly at Sandra, struggling to find my words. I couldn't think of a single thing to say to her. She lit a cigarette and blinked as the smoke rose up into her eyes. Then she smiled at me. "How old are you kid?" she asked.

"Nineteen." I lied. I didn't want her to know anything about me.

"You're not married then?" I shook my head. "We're not either," she giggled. "Well at least not to each other. Waiting for my divorce, you see." She started weaving her gaze away from me, observing the other drinkers who had crowded into the tiny bar. "Married to a copper I was. Derek Atkinson, a right tight arse an' all."

The mention of his name made me feel even worse than I was already, 'what next, don't say he's going to show up as well?' Lucky for me it was Magenta whom I saw swaggering towards us, with her customary dark shades and dark hair tied back. I was very relieved to see her.

As we approached the Carlton Hotel in our dilapidated charabanc, I felt the tension begin to rise up inside me. There was obviously some huge commotion happening outside the entrance and part way down the boulevard too. I could see a posse of photographers and white limousines, with crowds of onlookers clinging to them. There was a real buzz in the air and all around. On the beach opposite, there was even a temporary outdoor gymnasium. There were several, big muscled, bronzed guys, pumping weights. It looked like a mad-cap circus. Perhaps being dressed like a clown wasn't such a stupid mistake after all.

"All this diversion is going to be very helpful," announced Bryn.

"What are all these people doing here?" asked Sandra. I'd been wondering about that myself.

"It's the start of the annual Cannes film festival," said Magenta knowingly. "We're going to have to park up on a back street and walk into the hotel a different way. There must be a side entrance open to the hotel guests."

The inside of the hotel foyer was just as chaotic as the pathway leading up to the front entrance. The cavernous space was unrecognisable from just over a week ago. Practically all the golden, palatial opulence was now hidden behind a guard of honour of film posters and life size cardboard cut outs of famous film characters. There were even film star lookalikes: a Marilyn here and a Gable there, dotted about with trays full of champagne glasses to welcome the influx of VIP's. We were able to sneak in without too much fuss or attention being eyed upon us. Most of the big, uniformed bouncers were keeping a check on the main revolving door. Bryn rolled his right arm, like a policeman directing traffic, beckoning us to follow. I shrugged my shoulders towards Magenta. Bryn's thatch of red hair towered forwards as we followed, behind a throng of hotel guests, into the open, lounge bar area. We found an empty table near the back of the room, working on the principle that the hotel waiters would take a long time to reach us. Besides, there were already a couple of hundred people inside and it gave me a mild sense of security. "Safety in numbers," as Bryn put it. He asked Magenta and me to scan the faces around us to see if we could spot 'Les Americains'. After a few minutes, scanning backwards and forwards, we spotted them. They were all sat close to the kitchen door, all except Marsha. I sat opposite Bryn, so that I could keep an eye on them, without them seeing me.

"Well, what's happening?" he said impatiently.

"They're all just sat having drinks," I said. "Still no Marsha though. Maybe she's out shopping or something." I looked at Magenta for support, but she only raised her eyebrows nonchalantly.

"Well, we can't 'stand to' all afternoon. I'm going to have to make a move before we're T.O'd."

"T.O'd?"

"Thrown Out," smiled Bryn. "You girls stay here. If they make a move for the lifts," Bryn flipped his head backwards to indicate our targets. "Magenta, you'll have to get to the fifth floor before them and warn us. Right Byrney, follow me."

I crossed my fingers at Magenta and followed Bryn. He squeezed through the standing guests, carving a path like a Baltic icebreaker. Once we reached the foot of the wide, carpeted stairway, he glanced around quickly and took the first three steps in one stride.

When we reached the fifth floor, it was like stepping into an out-of-hours museum, the corridor was completely silent and devoid of people. At one end I could see the double steel, sliding lift doors. Above the lift was a digital display: pink numbers, illuminated behind the purple coloured glass, with a matching, coloured arrow, indicating the direction of travel. Beyond, the corridor bent round to the right and out of sight. We found room 505 and Bryn tried the door handle. The door was locked.

"Right," said Bryn. "I'll go in and take a look. You stand somewhere, so that you can cover both the stairs and the lift. Got it? If anyone comes up you'll have to improvise. If it's one of the Americans - give two knocks on the door, twice in quick succession."

"S.I.G." I said. "Spectrum is green?" It was something I remembered from the TV programme, 'Captain Scarlett and the Misterons', but it failed to make an impression with Bryn. Instead, he only gave a half hearted smile and shook his head at my attempts to join in with his repertoire.

"I think I'd better do the acronyms, Byrney. You just concentrate on keeping your eyes peeled.

Bryn took the master key from his pocket and stepped inside, closing the door behind him. I was beginning to feel nervous again, now that I was alone in the corridor. The lift indicator was still stuck at zero - good. I walked down to the top of the stairs and listened - all quiet. Then I heard a door open behind me. I leant on the bannister rail and casually turned my head to the left, expecting to see an unknown guest emerging; it was Bryn. He closed the door in his own, inimitable way, gingerly. We met up, half way.

"Your bloody Marsha, is still inside," he whispered angrily.

"How come?" I cringed. "I mean what's she doing? Did she see you?"

Bryn raised his right hand to silence me. "She's taking a bath." 'Taking it where?' I thought, 'blimey, is nothing sacred?' I started to giggle with nerves.

"It's okay she didn't see me. But I still need to finish searching her wardrobes." I could see Bryn grasping his fists tightly together as he thought of a ploy. Seeing the way he was dressed, how he cut quite a stocky, athletic figure, clean shaven and smart, and seeing the film star lookalikes downstairs, had given me an idea.

"Wait there, I'll be back in two ticks," I said as I raced back down the stairs.

After less than five minutes, I was standing back on the fifth floor corridor with Magenta. Together we had grabbed an empty tray and two glasses of champagne. I could see Bryn was less than pleased.

"So what's this for?" He enquired, wagging a disgruntled finger at the glasses.

"Just a gimmick, you know, in case Marsha catches you. Take the tray with you and pretend to be James Bond. You look a dead ringer for Roger Moore. Just say it's compliments of the management, two Vodka Martinis, shaken not stirred." I winked confidently at him.

Bryn took the tray and two glasses and hesitated. "Are you sure about this?" Magenta backed me up with, "You're a knock out, Bryn." He stepped back inside and left the door slightly ajar. We looked at each other and tried our best to stop ourselves from laughing out loud.

"He's funny, your friend," she said.

Our nerves were sharply steadied when we heard a few splashes being emitted from the bathroom, followed by a thump as one of the wardrobe doors closed. Then we heard Marsha's shrill voice, " Is that you Don?" The bathroom door opened. Through the narrow gap in the bedroom door we could see Marsha emerge wrapped in a bath sheet. "Who the hell are you?" She asked in Bryn's direction.

"The names Bond, James Bond. Can I offer you a drink?" Bryn said smoothly in a strange Lancashire Scots accent.

"Shaken or stirred, ma'am?"

"Oh my dear. How marvellous."

Poor Bryn we thought. The ploy was going too well.

"Compliments of the hotel management, ma'am." We could hear Bryn's voice getting closer as he made his way to the door. We turned away and quickly headed towards the lift doors. As Bryn exited the room, we could hear Marsha finishing her conversation with James Bond, "You're welcome to stay a while."

We all hid out of sight around the corner of the corridor. This time it was Bryn's turn to laugh. "That was a close shave."

"What about the jewels, did you find them?" Asked Magenta, bringing us back down to the task in hand.

Bryn shook his head despondently then stuck it carefully back down the open corridor.

"The coast is still all clear. Which room next do you think, 504 or 506?"

"I'm pretty certain Roger's in 506. Probably more chance with him than the sweet old couple Bill and Vivienne," I said.

We watched Bryn disappear further down the corridor again, unlocking the next bedroom door. Behind us, we heard the lift motor start up and turned to observe the ascending sequence of pink numbers: one, two, three, four. The higher up they went, the further we backed away from the doors. Whoever it was inside, they were now heading for the fifth and final floor. We stopped outside room 506 and turned to face each other. I raised my right arm and rested it high on the doorframe and whispered to Magenta as the lift doors slowly opened.

"Just pretend we're together."

Magenta placed her right hand on my shoulder and watched me closely while I tried to keep a look out, to see which direction the two guests were heading. They were a fabulous looking, young couple. The man was carrying a briefcase and the girl slinked past, barefooted and carrying her stiletto heeled shoes over her shoulder. She tutted at us in a mimicry way, softly saying, "Young lovers."

Our heads were touching. As soon as they'd closed their bedroom door, the door in front of us opened.

"Bulls eye, I've found them." whispered a wide-eyed Bryn. "Come and have a look." He led us into the sumptuously decorated room. The tall velvet curtains, stretching from floor to ceiling, were drawn back from the window, letting in floods of light, and noise too. One half of the pair of tall windows was open, revealing a decorative, wrought iron railing, guarding the drop to the palm trees that lined the noisy boulevard below. Bryn leant inside the wardrobe and passed me a white pair of leather brogue shoes. "Take a look inside?"

I tipped the shoes backward and out slid Marsha's sparkling necklace, earrings and broach. The light inside the room seemed to dance and dazzle. The diamonds were the size of marbles. Actually, they were almost the size of dobbers, king size marbles. "Wow, well done Bryn." I said, drooling at the sight of such beautiful objects. "What do we do now?"

"Give them to me."

I froze for a moment and looked at him thinking he was about to double cross us and take the jewels for himself. I reluctantly handed them back to him. "We'll put them back inside the wardrobe for now, then call the Gendarmes," he said.

"Wait a minute. Let me take a photo." I took out Fionn's little, pocket instamatic camera.

"Do you want me in on the photo too?" asked Bryn.

"Yer, why not."

It proved to be a lot trickier than we'd imagined, getting the Gendarmes to act on our information. I think they were puzzled by what a motley looking crew we were, and, found it difficult to believe we'd been let into the Carlton Hotel at all. The senior gendarme was sceptical with Bryn's story, that he'd found the door to room 506 had been left unlocked.

"We suspect you broke into the room to steal something?" It was all they kept repeating. Eventually, we asked to speak to the officer in charge. Luckily he recognised Magenta and me from the day he'd taken statements from everyone on board the Liberty Angel. "So now you want to play detective?" He was as equally unbelieving as the rest of them. He told us to wait inside the police station and he would check out our story. And if the jewels were still inside room 506, then of course we could claim the reward from the insurance company.

No doubt we were all in for a long wait. The wait was made all the worse watching Bryn pace backwards and forwards. Maybe he was feeling anxious too about being held in a French police station again, putting himself at their disposal. Still at least he wasn't being as demanding as Sandra, who moaned constantly about how she could murder a drink. Magenta, who was sat by my side, began speaking to me in French. Firstly asking how I'd picked up such a good understanding of it. I wasn't as proficient as she was, but I was proud of how much I'd improved during my time working with Anna, at Hotel Coraline in Saint Jean-les-Bains. I relayed to her the story of our 'liaisons amoureuse' and how I'd recently just discovered it was all over between Anna and me.

As we spoke Bryn and Sandra looked at us suspiciously. It felt very intimate to be conferring with Magenta in such a secretive and incomprehensible way, within earshot of our two collaborators.

After an hour the Police Inspector returned with some good news. He had contacted the insurance agent, who was at this precise moment making his way here to take our statements.

"And the jewels have been recovered?" Asked Bryn.

"Yes they are being kept in the hotel safe at the Carlton. We have arrested Monsieur Roger Martin on suspicion of stealing them. The other Americans in his party have checked out and moved into the Miramar, until we decide if we need to make any further arrests."

"And the reward?" Asked Sandra.

"Yes, the insurance agent will write out a bankers draft. I presume you all want an equal share?"

Sandra was clapping her hands with excitement. I looked at Magenta and said I wasn't interested. Bryn could have my five hundred dollars.

"In that case, he can have mine too," offered Magenta. "I didn't do anything really and besides I'm just happy to clear Fionn's good name."

"Yer, that goes for me too." I agreed.

This development put the biggest, broadest grin on Bryn's face. I don't actually think he was in it for the money either. He just wanted to prove to Sandra that he was a better detective than her ex husband. But there was no way Sandra was going to give up her share.

When we went our separate ways, I promised to meet up with Bryn at Rosie's Bar, the next evening, after the grand prix had finished. I suggested to Magenta that we should be heading back, otherwise we'd be locked out of the marina. But she wasn't ready for going back to Monte Carlo. "What about staying with your handsome French friend in Nice?"

"You mean Patrice?"

"Yes, who else? He's really good looking."

I agreed to call in there on our way back. I felt like I'd let him down the last time we'd seen him, when we collected Fionn. It would be really good to catch up with him for a while. He was such great company to be around, especially with his knowledge of music and the stories he knew about Eve when she had lived next door at Les Moulins, before and during the war.

As it turned out, it was a fantastic evening. We all had such a great time, the three of us. Patrice was very welcoming as usual. As the evening wore on I became aware that Patrice was the sort of guy who wore his heart on his sleeve and not surprisingly, he and Magenta really hit it off together. They shared the same personality and the same sense of humour. I wasn't sure how it would work between them, sex wise, knowing that Patrice was gay and Magenta was one foxy lady, as she pointed out to us, while dancing along to the Jimi Hendrix song of the same name. During the course of the many conversations we had whilst we rifled through his record collection, it all came out about what had occurred at the Col de la Celeste, when Patrice and Bryn had been shot. "This was the guy who's been helping us find the missing jewels." She scowled at me. "I knew there was more to it than him being just a family friend," she exclaimed. "You sneaky sod."

I was expecting her to drop me like a stone after she learnt, too, about the robbery at Crowston Post Office. But Patrice defended me to her, coming to my rescue and faithfully restoring my reputation, by saying how I'd given all the money away to a good cause, hunting Nazis who were on the run.

"My god Byrney, you're a dark knight in disguise."

I begged her not to say anything to the other crew members, especially Fionn and she agreed.

Patrice offered to put us both up for the night. "You two can sleep down here on separate sofas, if you like?"

I reminded Magenta again about being unable to get back inside the fenced off marina, with all the additional security checks that would be in place by morning. But Magenta was one cool step ahead of me, saying she knew of a way back to our vessel, which didn't go near the racetrack.

After Patrice retired up to his mezzanine, we both made up our beds for the night. I watched Magenta undress down to her underwear and settle on her sofa, with just a cotton sheet for a cover. As she watched me fumbling about, unfolding my cover, she smiled at me, saying, "You can climb in here with me."

We talked into the early hours of the morning, just the two of us, but I was struggling to keep my eyes open. The beers we'd drunk earlier were taking their toll on my concentration. Magenta was telling me about her father, Ramon de Cruz. He'd been a diplomatic in Portugal during the Second World War and had helped refugees and displaced persons, with transit letters to far off destinations, like United States of America, Canada and Great Britain. I must have nodded off for a moment. "Come on Byrney, our little, cosy chat is over. You'd better move across to your own bed now. I need to get some sleep too."

When the first rays of sunlight poured into Patrice's studio, it was time for us to slip away. Watching Magenta dress again was just as spell binding as watching her undress the night before. Although we'd both only had a few hours sleep, it felt strangely like a totally different day. Then I remembered it was Sunday, race day.

It was as if we were the only ones alive, as we twisted around the lonely rocky coast road, back to the marina in Cap d'Ail. We had the windows down, with the cassette player turned up as high as the vibrating speakers allowed, listening to the Rumours album. 'Open your eyes, look at the day and you'll see things in a different way."

Indeed, summer was beginning to happen and in my opinion I was in one of the greatest places on earth. Magenta drove straight round to the little restaurant at the end of the quayside opposite our old, permanent mooring in the quiet marina.

"Pascal's normally out and about at this hour," she said, smiling from behind her dark shades. "I know he's got a little motor boat, which he uses every week to go to the market in Ventimiglia. He won't mind ferrying us around the headland to Monte Carlo. He owes me a few favours."

And that was how we came to be stepping back across the Liberty Angel gangplank at seven a.m. on the day of the Monaco grand prix, before any of our fellow crew members had risen, before anyone realised we hadn't been on board all night and just in time to make breakfast for our few remaining guests.

Having grabbed an extra four hours sleep inside my cabin, I was woken by the roar of noise from the spectators in the nearby grandstand.

Fionn was just coming back over the gangplank as I surfaced from below, with a cup of black coffee.

"You've missed half the fun already," she teased, beaming from ear to ear. "Princess Grace and Prince Rainier have just driven all the way around the racetrack in an open top Rolls Royce. I was standing ever so close to them when they passed. Princess Grace even waved at me. She's so beautiful, even though she's older than my mum."

I did my best to look enthusiastic and shake the sleep from my eyes. Fionn gave me a hug and said, "That's for helping to find the jewels and clear my name. Magenta told me all about it this morning." I had a flash of nerves, wondering what else had been said. Then Fionn blurted out, "Why the hell didn't you keep the reward money? We could have had a great party, all of us."

I scratched my head, thinking of how to change the subject. "Yer I never thought of that." I said lamely. "We were both wrong in the end, about who'd taken Marsha's jewels. Who would have thought it'd be that shy Roger who'd nicked them."

"Well, I never really trusted him," revealed Fionn. "His ears were far too close together."

"Don't you mean, his eyes, Fi?"

Looking out towards the racetrack and the hills and tall buildings beyond, it was such a colourful spectacle, despite the sun being mostly obscured by white clouds. However, nothing could overshadow the excitement that lay in store. Strewn across the hillside opposite was a patchwork of flags and banners. The majority of the ones with the best viewpoints were from Italy. This was not surprising, as they only had to hop over the border from thirty miles further up the Cote d'Azur. But, they were by far the noisiest and most patriotic race fans, with their bright red Ferrari flags in constant motion. No doubt they would be cheering for their men in the hot seats: Niki Lauda and Carlos Reutemann.

I made my way over to the outside of the wire mesh, perimeter fencing, just in front of the port chicane as planned. I stood next to a few strangers. Al and Gareth were still sat on board with the Champion marketing people, watching the race on the ship's television in the salon lounge. 'How crazy,' I thought. I was determined to soak up the atmosphere and get as close to the action as possible. Before the race started, Martin appeared, with two cans of coke.

"Cheers, do you think James Hunt will win?" I asked.

"I can't see it happening today," he said with all sincerity. "He's well down on the grid and overtaking here is almost impossible."

The noise of the engines as the racing cars set off was deafening. The angry, roaring sound rebounded from the tall buildings and echoed down to the sea front. Although we could only see a small part of the track, when the first cars emerged from the tunnel to our right, I couldn't believe how fast they were going. There was barely a car's length between them as they twisted left and right through the tight chicane. And this was meant to be a slow part of the circuit. I noticed one or two of the drivers were unable to slow down in time to turn into the first corner, opting instead for a short run off area that had been put in place for such emergencies and mistakes.

The spectators to my left, in the make shift seated area just a few yards away, all stood up and cheered every time the race leaders went past. The race continued at such a relentless, frantic pace, but as Martin had predicted it was turning into a procession. The English fans had little to cheer about. James Hunt retired early and the Irishman, John Watson, who'd lead the race for a while, also failed to finish. The eventual winner was the South African driver, Jody Scheckter. The Italian hopeful finished second, so at least most of the fans from the other side of the Riviera went home happy.

By six p.m., my lack of sleep from the previous night was beginning to catch up with me. I knew I had to say farewell to Bryn, so I was hoping he'd be sat at the bar in the early part of the evening too. Lucky for me he was.

When we parted, after just one drink, it was as good friends. And all the ill feelings from our previous encounters of last year were, thankfully, long forgotten. I'd managed to get over the initial shock of finding him in my favourite French pub three days ago. Somehow, I'd set myself up too, into getting into cahoots with this guy, whom I knew had the power to crush me with his bare hands. And going after the jewels turned out to be just one of the lesser, sticky situations we'd been through together, only this time, we managed to get the right result. We sank the last drops of our beers and wished one another good luck with our ventures, Bryn offering to stand me a pint or two at the Bulls Head in Churchtown, the next time I was home.

And with a smart military about turn, he marched out of the door.

"T.T.F.N. Byrney."

"T.T.F.N. Bryn."

Chapter Six

'Quando Il Sole Tramonta'

Part One

Breakfast, the following morning, overran the usual thirty minutes, mainly because we had the ship to ourselves. We took full advantage of this, by treating ourselves to the large circular oak table, on the aft deck. Although it was only eight-thirty a.m, the mercury on the nearby thermometer was already reading sixty-five degrees Fahrenheit. Captain Al was in full flow, regaling us with one of his many tales from 'a life on the ocean wave'. He looked even more like a pirate these days, having grown a 'full set' since his trip to Naples, and his shiver-m'-timbers, grizzly appearance served to further enhance his stories. Apart from dozy Dave, I wasn't sure anyone actually believed them all or not, but we all found them hugely entertaining. The tale we were currently captivated by, had happened around four years ago, when Al had been chartering in warmer waters, along the Red Sea coastline.

"The diving there is probably the best in the world. The coral reefs are fantastic - teeming with fish and wildlife, and some of it not so friendly, like the occasional hammer head or tiger shark."

"I've heard you get poisonous sea snakes there too," interrupted Dave, enthusiastically.

"Actually, Dave, there are no snakes in the Red Sea. The things that most divers believe to be snakes are actually eels. True, some are venomous, but mostly they're quite shy and harmless."

Dave looked a bit crest fallen, but no one else noticed.

"There's some fantastic wrecks down there though, in quite shallow water," continued Al. "great for exploring, like the SS Thistledown, bombed by the Germans and sunk in 1941, with lots of ordnance on board. It even has some old cars and lorries too, all still perfectly intact, inside the hold. The Thistledown wreck was first discovered by Jacques Cousteau. You'll have all heard of him, no doubt. He even managed to salvage one of the World War Two motorbikes."

"Did he get it running?" asked Dave without thinking.

"I doubt it. The engine would've been full of sea water, you twit."

While we were all laughing, Magenta came through from the kitchen, with another, full cafetière of black coffee. Fionn followed her, carrying a basket of fresh croissants. They'd obviously already been out earlier, to the boulangerie, near the old Rascasse restaurant.

No one was aware, that I'd also been out for a walk, at first light, around five-thirty a.m. I was intrigued by the deserted race track in the dawn light: the empty grandstands, the discarded litter, flotsam and jetsam that had gathered into windswept spoil heaps. I wasn't alone for long before the street cleaners and technicians emerged, equipped to restore the roadway and pavements for the sleeping tourists. It was an opportune moment to take some interesting photos. I'd purposefully saved a few, unused exposures to record what I thought to be the bare bones of a grand prix circuit, after the champagne bubbles had evaporated.

Whilst we chomped through our plump, flaky croissants, Al was still Red Sea reminiscing.

"Back in '73, there was a fair sized armada of big tankers laid up along the Persian Gulf, due to the oil crisis. I remember one in particular, an old T2 tanker. We used to pass it every day, just off Sharm El-Sheikh. It looked completely deserted, but there was this old Palestinian guy stuck on there, all alone. The oil company had left him on board to keep an eye on the ship. Even stationary ships need to be looked after. Anyway, one day he was leaning over the handrail, shouting for help. He spoke quite good English. I was curious and he looked fairly innocuous, so I pulled up alongside and he invited me on."

"What if he'd had a gun or tried to kidnap you?" asked Fionn, anxiously.

"As it happens, he did have a gun, mainly for protection though. When I got chatting with him, he was anxious to let me know there was no electrical power on board and consequently nothing worked, including the radio."

"Poor guy," said Fionn, changing her tune.

"I borrowed a torch and we went down five decks to the engine room. It was like being inside a steel coffin, eerily quiet. I eventually located the generator, which had obviously stopped running a long time ago. All I did was change the fuel filter, prime the pump and it started straight away. The little Palestinian guy was over the moon. He invited me back the next day and he cooked us a lovely meal. Trev was with me then too," Al recalled.

"You should write a book Al," said Fionn, who'd been thoroughly enthralled. "What a story."

Before Al could reply, Gareth leant forward and said he'd been recently thinking about writing a book. "I'm going to call it, The Curse of the Big Nobs."

"What, you got a big nob then?" asked Dave, making Fionn blush.

"No, I'm not saying that. Well, not that I've had any complaints so far," he boasted. "No, actually it's more about the curse than the actual size."

"What's the curse then?" asked Dave, showing a slightly unhealthy interest.

"Well, since you've asked, it's about a guy whose brain is controlled by his old chap." We all began to laugh again.

"You mean, like most men are," said Magenta dryly.

"Right, come on you lot. Back on your heads," ordered Al and further clapping his hands for emphasis. "Remember, we have to leave Monte, today. Otherwise, the additional mooring fees will be coming out of your wages, if old man Bailey has anything to do with it."

That afternoon, we left the harbour and instead of turning right as usual back to Cap d'Ail - we turned left and headed for San Remo in Italy, forty miles further up the coast.

It felt very comforting to be back on the move again, even in the noisy, smelly, smoky environs of the old engine room. Even the engines seemed to purr with pleasure - we must be treating them kindly, I thought.

"Al's decided we need to do some bunkering," said Martin as he documented the details of our present journey in the engine room log-book.

"What's that?" I asked

"Bunkering? Refuelling to you and me," he said with his head still bent over his writing. " Fuel prices are cheaper in Italy and duty free, as we're crossing into another country. Al will probably be down soon, to see if you want any duty free booze picking up from the port store."

"Not sure 'bout that. You getting anything?"

"Normally buy some Bacardi, tastes nice with ice and coke," he smiled.

"Okay, I'll do the same."

Bunkering in San Remo was an uneventful process. We moored up 'alongside', against the pale, concrete, quayside on the main harbour wall, right next to a garage style fuel pump. Surely not, I thought, looking at the narrow hose. Luckily, we were connected up to a mobile fuel bowser as our tanks held around four thousand gallons. Glad I wasn't paying for it. Captain Al kept a strong box, full of petty cash, locked away in the wheelhouse. It was the only form of payment, which the Italians accepted.

About an hour later, when the bunkering was done, Al and Magenta returned to the ship, each carrying a cardboard box full of various bottled spirits. My bottle of Bacardi cost me twenty francs, about two quid in old money.

By the time we arrived back at our usual berth in Cap d'Ail marina, our manoeuvres took longer than normal before the 'finished with engines' signal was rung down. We'd been instructed to find an alternative mooring as there was another large motor yacht occupying our usual space. Our new port side neighbour, we soon learnt, was one of the four other company ships owned by Liberty Yachts. The Liberty Princess was the grandest and largest.

"One hundred and seventy-five feet long," said Martin as we gazed at our big sister. "And that outranks ours by forty foot."

As we stood on the poop deck, admiring her vintage, streamlined curves, we couldn't help but be impressed. Down both the port and starboard sides ran a part covered, gangway decking, which was something our ship sadly lacked. She was much taller and longer at the bow too, which rose from the waterline, almost to a razor sharp point. We noticed a couple of her deck-hands faffing about, adjusting the fenders. They wore the same white uniforms as us, and on their feet, the same, cheap leather deck shoes. No doubt their toes were dyed blue, just like ours.

I could see Al had wasted no time in strolling up their gang plank to welcome our visiting stable mates to France.

"That's Eric Tyler, the captain," said Martin, pointing out a chubby, grey haired man in a grubby, white, short-sleeved shirt, worn with black and gold bands in the shoulder epaulettes, to signify his superior rank. "Apparently, Eric and Al go back a long way. I had a bit of a Liberty Yachts history lesson during my interview in Barry last year," he recalled. "Al used to be Eric's first mate, when they crewed together on the first Liberty Yacht - The Liberty Queen."

I watched the two men greet one another with a bear hug and several hard slaps over one another's shoulders. The chubby guy appeared to stagger, like he'd been drinking already.

"Yes, he's well known for it," confirmed Martin.

The more I watched captain Eric address his deck hands, with shouts and sharp commands, the more my gut feeling said I should keep my distance.

When we were all invited on board for drinks, later that evening, I made my excuses to remain aboard The Angel. I was accused by Dave of being a wet nelly, when I told him I was popping into town to make some phone calls. It takes one to know one, I thought.

For the first time in a while, I was beginning to feel homesick. It'd been well over six months since I'd last seen my parents and our Anthony. In the little telephone kiosk, opposite Rosie's bar, mum's voice came through on the other end of the line. She sounded so loud and clear, just like she was standing next to me. I could hear her excited breath when she paused to listen to the tales about what I'd been up to and the places I'd seen so far.

They'd decided to put our mobile home up for sale, at the end of the school term. Mum had been offered a new post in Skipton, North Yorkshire, with the same fashion house she worked for in Lancaster. "I'll be able to see more of my brother and your nanna. She's getting a little frailer these days and needs someone who's around more to help her out. So we're going to move in with her for a while, until we find a place of our own."

"Are you sure that's a good idea, Mum?" I knew how much dad and uncle Ray used to argue, whenever they were together for longer than five minutes. It was lovingly referred to by dad as 'The War of the Roses', but it was mostly just about cricket.

"Don't worry about your father. He'll soon come around to the idea, once he's caught a glimpse of how many pubs there are in Skipton."

When I put down the receiver, I was actually feeling more sad and unsettled than I was before. I had no excuse or opportunity now for going back to The Friary. It was so easy to lose touch with people back home, especially when back home was about to move fifty miles in the wrong direction. True, most of my schoolmates had already moved away too, into further education, or family businesses. And I'd already lost track of most of them. Luckily, I still had one great friend with me from school - Fionn.

I looked at the crowd of people gathered inside Rosie's Bar and gave myself a little pep talk. "Hey, come on Byrney, summer's almost here."

Whenever we had a short gap between charters, Al normally let us come and go as we pleased, provided everything was ship shape and hunky dory. Today, most of the crew were nursing hangovers, after the inter-Liberty party aboard The Princess, the previous evening. Besides our two girls and me, Gareth was the only other crew member showing any signs of life.

"How do you fancy learning to water ski, Byrney?" Sounded like an excellent idea to me. "Al agreed last night into letting me take the Riva for a run out, to keep her batteries charged up and everything."

Fionn and Magenta were both just as enthused to come along for the ride too. "Okay let's get moving before anyone else wakes up. Otherwise they'll all want to come along and four's the perfect number."

"We'll put some things together for a picnic," suggested Magenta while helping Fionn to clear away breakfast.

I looked at them and smiled. "I'll get my trunks on."

Within fifteen minutes, Gareth had removed a section of the handrail on the boat deck and had swung the davit arm over the side. He sat inside the speedboat whilst I lowered him into the water at our starboard side, out of view of our Liberty neighbour. After unclipping the steel cables, he pushed the Riva along with his hands until he reached the bottom of the wooden side steps. The girls were waiting on the bottom step as I rushed down to follow them into the little red boat. It was already loaded with skis, picnic basket and a cool bag, by the time I clambered inside.

At the last moment, Gareth pressed the starter button, put her into forward gear and we idled clear of the hull, chugging quietly out of the marina at the head of a gentle, disappearing wake, until we passed beyond the rocky harbour wall. We headed out into the bay in the direction of nearby Plage

Marquet, a favourite sun spot. The still sea was completely empty of bathers.

The tiny glass screen above the steering wheel offered no shelter from the cool breeze as we roared further out. I looked round at the four of us. Everyone's hair was dancing like a whirling dervish and every now and again a splash of sea spray fanned over the curved, rear bench seat, making us laugh. Once we were about half a mile from shore, Gareth throttled back and put the gearbox in neutral and quickly looked around. "Ideal conditions for a beginner," he said confidently. "Okay, who wants to go first?"

In the short pause that followed, I stood up and said, "Okay, what do I have to do." I was a good swimmer and not afraid of water. I never gave it a single thought as to how deep it was. I already knew it was far too deep to touch the bottom of the sea bed when I jumped in the water, but it was cooler than I expected. Magenta passed me the pair of skis. I could tell by the elated expression on her face she thought I was about to make a fool of myself. I'd already almost jumped in without taking my t-shirt off first, in my eagerness.

"Okay, put your skis on and sit in the water with your knees together, bent up against your chest," continued Gareth. I did as I was instructed and the tips of my skis rocked from side to side above the surface of the water as I tried to keep them straight. Magenta leant over the stern and handed me the wooden handle that was attached to the end of the line. I was beginning to wish I'd let someone else go first so that I could see how it was supposed to be done. And I was going to have to get used again to the taste of the sea.

"You okay Byrney? Try and keep your ski's straight." Hollered Gareth as the boat drew away slowly. "When you see the line go tight, brace yourself. Don't fight it. When you feel the line lift out of the water, just try and stand up."

I normally prided myself with having good balance, but the tips of my ski's were still rocking in all directions. I noticed Magenta and Fionn both giving me encouraging waves. Fionn also had her camera poised.

"Oh, and one last thing Byrney, when you stand up at first, you'll feel the line go slack. Whatever you do, don't bend your arms and pull the line towards you. The best thing to do is to keep both your arms straight out in front of you and raise the line in the air." Gareth gave a little demonstration.

"Come on. Get on with it," said Magenta. "We all want a go too, you know."

Gareth sat down in the drivers seat and gave me a signal. "Here goes - hold tight."

My skis were still rocking, but as I heard the engine rev up and felt the line tighten, they were pulled together. I felt a sharp tug on the line and I gritted my teeth. In the same instant that the line tried to break away from me, I began to climb out of the water and my legs straightened. I was up. I couldn't believe it. Then the line slackened and I began to lean too far over, backwards. I pulled the line towards me, but it was too late. Instead of falling backwards, the line pulled me forwards again, face first, under the waves, head skiing. After a few yards, I let go. When I surfaced again, I could hear everyone laughing. I looked around, recovered my composure and my ski's, ready for a fresh attempt.

When Gareth brought the Riva back around he said it wasn't bad for my first go, but I'd just forgotten about the line. He demonstrated the move once more, raising his arms. "Ready to go again?"

"Yer, I'm enjoying this." I wasn't entirely sure if I was or not. I was beginning to think I was out of my depth, literally. "Are there any sharks in the Med?" I asked.

"Not on a weekday. There aren't enough tourists to eat," cracked Gareth,

"Very funny," I said, squirting another fountain of salty water from my mouth.

Magenta handed me the line. "Nice try Byrney, almost perfect."

When the line pulled me free from the deep a second time, I made no mistake. Lifting the line as high as it allowed and I was actually skiing. This time everyone cheered and waved. From the rear of the boat the foaming wake was incredibly flat and broad. 'Wow what do I do now?' I thought, 'just hang on, I guess.'

We jetted along in a wide arc and after what seemed like ages to me, but was probably only three of four minutes in reality, I realised I needed shock absorbers for legs and shoulders and mine were beginning to ache like hell. Having surrendered the line, I glided to a halt with a definite sinking feeling. The boat ambled back alongside and Gareth helped to drag me back on board.

"Wow, that was different. Easy-peasy, once you get the hang of it."

"Well done." Cheered Fionn. "I'm not sure I'll be that good."

"Do you want to go next?" Asked Gareth.

"Not just yet," she said, shyly. "I'll let Magenta go before me."

I sat next to Gareth for a close up look at how he handled the Riva. I was dying to have a go at piloting, more so than learning how to ski.

Magenta tied her hair back into a bob and slipped gracefully into the sea, then immediately tipped one of the skis back inside the boat. "I won't be needing that one."

At the first attempt, she emerged like one of Homer's classic Greek goddesses. I watched her lean backwards, perfectly balanced, letting the line do all the work as she veered out from the foaming wake and into the shiny flat surface at the side. When she was almost ninety degrees to our stern, she leant over to her side and let the line pull her straight across to the opposite side, bouncing over the two rims of our wake. She was making it look so easy. I could tell Fionn was having second thoughts.

"God she's good. I'm not sure I'll be able to follow on from that."

Gareth suggested we swap seats and he let me steer for a while. "Always turn to the opposite side to where Magenta is heading." I looked behind me and saw that Magenta was still hanging on. After a short while, she eased back into the centre of the wake and signalled that she was pulling up, then let go of the line. Gareth throttled right back and I steered alongside. "Whenever you're manoeuvring, always have the throttle set on idle. That way it's easier to correct any mistakes. You have to remember there are no brakes to slow you down."

"Okay, Roger that." I said in mock agreement.

"Do you want me to take the next turn on the skis?" He asked, aiming his question at Fionn.

"Yes, okay. I don't mind waiting."

"Okay Byrney, I'll raise my arm when I'm ready. Just put the gearbox in forward gear and open up the throttle smoothly to about half way, will be fine."

Magenta was wiping her face with a towel as Fionn handed Gareth the line. I pulled forward gently until I could see the line lift up out of the sea as it began to reach its full tension. Gareth quickly raised his hand and I opened up the throttle. I glanced back to see Gareth following behind, congratulating himself with a few 'woohoo's'.

There were no acrobatics from him. He stayed in the centre of the wake for his full five minute run. When he climbed back into the hull of our boat, he hauled both ski's back inside too.

"Nice one Byrney."

I shrugged my shoulders like I'd just become an instant expert.

"Well, what's it to be Fionn. Fancy a go?"

She was put on the spot and she knew there was no way of avoiding the issue any longer. "Okay, I'll give it a go."

"Yeah, go girl, that's the spirit," said Magenta, encouragingly.

I handed the wheel back to Gareth, thinking a more experienced pilot would give Fionn a better chance of success. Magenta went through the full instructions again for Fionn's benefit, but she still wasn't sure. So Magenta slipped back into the sea beside her.

As the line ran out to its full length, I could see both their heads bobbing about in the water. The sea wasn't quite a still as it had been earlier in the morning. After two more minutes of floating in neutral, Magenta eventually waved her arm aloft, but as soon as the line reached it full tension it sprang loose again as Fionn let go of the handle. I could see she was having trouble keeping the tips of her ski's clear of the surface. Her next attempt was virtually a repeat of her first. At the third attempt, Fionn rose partially out of the water and was being pulled along in a seated position skimming the waves,

"Stand up," waved Gareth.

After a few more yards, to our amazement, Fionn managed to straighten her legs and was stood upright. However, it was only a short run, less than two minutes before she lost her balance and plunged headlong into the sea.

She was still laughing when we picked her up, having collected Magenta first along the way.

"Think I've got salt water up my bum," laughed Fionn as she slumped into the hull of the boat. We all gave her a well earned round of applause.

"Let's head over to the beach and have some grub. I'm starving," announced Gareth as he gunned the Riva over to the empty shoreline at Plage Marquet.

When we returned to our mooring, I'd forgotten about the Liberty Princess being moored beside us. With her steep angled brow there was no argument about which of our two boats was the most imposing. I much preferred it when we had the marina to ourselves. I didn't mind sharing with the smaller craft, the speedboats and the cigars as Gareth called them. It was obvious, from the difference in size between our two Liberty motor yachts, which of these was boss.

Al was waiting anxiously for us by the starboard side steps. For a moment, I thought we were about to be reprimanded for disappearing most of the day with the Riva. Then I noticed the slovenly figure of the captain of the Liberty Princess, lurking in the shadows of our aft deck.

"Eric wants to have a run out in the Riva," explained Al.

"Does he want me to take him?" Asked Gareth.

"No, that won't be necessary. I can handle a speedboat." Retorted Eric as he stepped into view.

We watched the Riva speed away with the same feeling as if we'd just been mugged by someone, stealing our prized possession. Al spoke apologetically. "You might as well know. Eric's asked me if he can loan the Riva for the remainder of the season." We all complained.

"Look, it's out of my hands. Besides, it's more suited to their business portfolio. They're mainly booked to do day trips. And water-skiing is a large proportion of their itinerary." Al looked amongst our disheartened faces as we turned to walk away. "But, there is some good news. We've been given their next charter. So at the end of this week, we'll be hosting a top Italian film crew." We looked at each other with a 'might not be so bad' sort of approval as Al continued. "They're going to be shooting some scenes on board and around St. Tropez. Real film stars, guys." Then, looking at Magenta, he said, "You've always wanted to be in the movies. You never know, maybe now's your chance."

"Oh yer, anyone we might have heard of?" asked Gareth, still sounding slightly nonplussed.

"I'll let everyone know, once I get the details from Eric," He said as we trudged off back to our cabins, feeling deflated after such an ace day. "What a come down," I said out loud.

That night, it was the turn of the Liberty Angel to reciprocate the joint hospitality with the crew of our Liberty neighbours. So Al arranged to push two large tables together at Pascal's Restaurant, just a stone's throw away at the end of the quay.

"Not too far to stagger home," Gareth contentedly pointed out.

No matter how much Eric and Al tried to cement the harmony between the two crews, we were still clinging on to our own separate little groups. The Angel crew were holed up at one end of the table and the Princess lot at the other. Apart from Eric and Al who were sat facing each other, the only other 'cordialement' lay between our two girls and Dot, who was the chef aboard the Princess. The three of them occupied the next seats along from the two captains. But, from what I could make out of their awkward chit chat, Fionn and Magenta had drawn the short straw. Dot's sole topic of conversation began and ended with her boasting on about her Jersey passport. "With this I don't have to pay any tax."

"We don't have to pay any tax either," teased Fionn. "Mind you, we don't get any pay to begin with," she laughed.

As the food was passed around the table, Gareth, who was sat closest to the Princess crew, was attempting to put names to faces. Next to Dot was Derek Watson. He was Eric's second in command. Next to him, the guy with the really bad acne was Gregg Holmes, deckhand. "Face like a pizza topping," he whispered. Then, finally, there was Keith Fawcett, who they called Motty. Gareth must have noticed my puzzled expression. "I know," said Gareth in agreement. "Doesn't make any sense. I said this to him last night. Apparently when he joined the Princess crew last year, he had a black leather biker jacket with painted white lettering across the back of it with the word Mott. Short for Mott the Hoople. I think he's a deckhand too."

The beer that accompanied the food was being handed out faster than free tickets to a Rolling Stones concert, with the effect that our tongues became loose enough, to engage in conversation with the opposing crew. I mentioned to Gareth that they had a Holmes and Watson on board.

"Yeah, it's a bit of a coincidence in'it? We could have a few laughs with this," he said, smiling and then he stood up to face the crew at the opposite end of the table.

"So, Derek," shouted Gareth at Eric's second in command, grabbing everyone's attention. "I've just realised about the coincidence of your crew names." He turned and gave an exaggerated wink in our direction.

"Let me guess," replied Derek sarcastically. "You've worked it out. We've got a Holmes and Watson." The other Princess crew lads sniggered down their noses.

"No, I was thinking of something else actually," and he began to point to their faces in turn as he called out their names. "You've got: Dotty, Watty, Motty and you, Gregg, must be Spotty." It was at this precise moment, the punch up erupted.

In truth it had been simmering for a while and by the time we were eventually pulled apart by an angry Pascal and his two waiters, there was food everywhere: on our clothes, around the tables, on the floor, even floating in the sea.

With the situation having calmed down, we paid Pascal our dues and gave him our humble apologies. Then Eric and Al had us lined up like an I.D parade. They could probably have sacked us all on the spot, if Eric had a mind to do it. But being half cut himself, we were all let off with a verbal slurring and a warning.

Looking down the line of battered and food splattered bodies, Gareth had come off the worse. He'd taken two or three punches on his hooter. One of them had also accidentally come from Dave. Afterwards, it was decided we'd keep to our own vessels, for the rest of the week.

The next day turned out to be the worse day for me since I'd been in France. Even worse than the day Anna's dad had threatened to kill me and my companions, wounding two of us in the ensuing shoot out.

My worse day began by Martin confessing to me that he was jumping ship and joining the Liberty Princess. At first I thought he was winding me up.

"No, it's a great opportunity for me to progress. They have two Caterpillar V8 engines on board, much simpler, cleaner and quieter and more modern, of course. The engine room needs some reorganising, but I need a new challenge." I was really going to miss Martin. We'd been a good team just the two of us, working together. But, more than that, I'd come to look upon him as an older, more knowledgeable brother. He was still slightly vulnerable and shy, but maybe this was the right time for him to move on and improve.

"I don't suppose anything I say will get you to change your mind?"

"No it's all been agreed. I'm going to move my stuff over, later today." Then he handed me a brown paper bag. " I want you to have these." It was the white pair of Champion Spark Plug overalls, completely unworn.

"Wow, thanks Martin. You didn't have to." I said, gratefully accepting his gift. "I'll buy you a drink later." I wasn't expecting any of that.

Later in the afternoon, I popped into town to collect my photographs of the Monaco Grand Prix from the film processors. I knew Fionn was keen to see what I'd taken with her camera, so she joined me later in my cabin, so that we could open them together. I was interested too, in seeing how the photos of the empty racetrack had turned out – the ones I'd taken the morning after the race.

"Ooh I love looking at photographs, don't you?" she said, excitedly. I opened the sealed pack and we studied each one together. The first ones, of the formula one cars, during the practise session, weren't very successful. Some had just a wheel and some of the cars were missing altogether. The next photograph had nothing to do with the Grand Prix at all. I'd cleanly forgotten all about it. Before I could tuck it into the back of the pack, Fionn reached it from me.

It was the one I'd taken of Gingernut Bryn, in Roger Martin's room, holding Marsha's jewels. My heart was in my mouth. I tried to stop Fionn staring at it, by showing her the next photo.

"Look at this one Fi of the empty Grandstand."

"Just a minute, Byrney. Who's this big guy in the photo here, with what I presume are Marsha's stolen jewels?"

My mouth was completely dry. I struggled to think of an alternative explanation, less incriminating. "Just a guy," I said feebly, "Who helped to find them."

"Yes, but how do you know him?" She demanded.

"I don't really."

Fionn moved further away from me. "You're lying to me Byrney. I know who he is. He's the guy from the train."

"What train? What are you talking about?"

"The train from Preston down to London last October. He's the guy who was sat at the back when that fight broke out."

"Now you mention it, I suppose he looks similar."

"Don't lie to me Byrney. What's he doing here? I want to know the truth. I thought we were friends."

"We are Fi. Christ, you're my best friend." There was nothing else for it. I had to trust her. It would be better for me to tell her the whole story, rather than her hearing it from someone else. "I'm not sure you'll still want to be my friend after I tell you everything," I confessed.

I watched Fionn's expression change from disbelief to hurt and finally, to deep anger.

"You did all this and you never said a word. How could you? I put my complete trust in you, leaving the Friary. And all the time we've been together, you've been keeping the truth from me."

She stood up and slammed the door behind her, then instantly opened it again.

"I thought I knew you Byrney, you're no friend of mine."

I felt sick with devastation. Seeing how Fionn had reacted to what I'd done hurt me a thousand times more than the 'Dear John' letter I'd recently received from Anna. Fionn was my oldest friend. I deeply regretted not telling her until now. I was such a coward. Max had said it to me last year when we'd fought and she was right. I was a coward and it had knocked all the stuffing out of me. I was totally gutted.

I picked up the photo of Bryn with his cheesy smile and tore it to pieces. I couldn't see a way back from this now, at all.

Chapter Six

'Quando Il Sole Tramonta'

Part Two

It was time to face the music. I was never going to get away with lying in bed forever. I decided to give Fionn some breathing space. She was still sharing a cabin with Magenta, so I knew she wasn't exactly short of company.

Al collared me after breakfast, alone in the engine room. I was familiarising myself with the engine room log book and reading Martin's comments at the end of our last journey from San Remo. He'd signed off with, 'Good Luck to the Crew of the Liberty Angel - Happy Sailing'.

"You're probably wondering who's going to be manning the second engine now that Martin's left," said Al, interrupting my thoughts. Up until five minutes ago, I'd not given much time to wondering about that particular question - there were too many other 'disturbinations' lingering inside my mind. Al forced a smile and rested a hand on my shoulder. "I know it's a big ask for you to train someone new in the black art of driving the engines, but...."

'Oh no what's coming now,' I thought.

"I've every confidence in you. And I know you've been a match for Martin, even showing him a thing or two." I began to walk to the other side of the engine as he spoke, as if to create some space before his next sentence, like it was some kind of self-defence mechanism. But, Al tagged along close behind. "So here's the rub."

'Here we go,' I thought. 'He wants me to run both engines at once'.

"I've decided to put Dave down here with you."

Al must have seen the look of horror on my face. It was actually a worse outcome than working both engines alone.

"He's a good honest lad is Dave," blurted Al quickly. "I know he can be a bit backward at coming forward at times and let's face it, he's never going to make a deckhand. So it's the last chance lifeboat for Dave. If he can't hack it down here with you, it's goodnight Monte Carlo."

I felt like I'd been dropped right in it. Just when I thought things couldn't get any worse: first we lose the Riva, then Martin leaves, my best friend hates me and now, I've got Dopey Dave sat next to me, ten hours a day.

"Oh and one last thing Byrney, we're departing after lunch to rendez-vous with our Italian film crew."

Balls, I'd forgotten about them as well.

"Don't worry, we won't be tying up anywhere tricky for a while. We're anchoring in the Gulf of Grimaud, just opposite St. Tropez, until further notice."

When Dave joined me down in the engine room, about half an hour later, he had the biggest, cheekiest grin on his face. It was almost impossible for me to be angry with him. Dave was at least two or three years older than me physically, but mentally? That was a different story.

This was his second season on board. He'd joined the Liberty Angel towards the end of last year and to begin with everyone on board at the time was very wary of him, knowing he'd been given a deckhand job solely on the strength of being one of Al's distant relations. But, during those first few days, it soon became obvious, to all of them, that there was nothing underhand about Dave. According to Gareth, Dave's first job had been sweeping the decks and instead of collecting up the rubbish in a dustpan, he'd swept it over the side. The rubbish fell on top of Gareth who was sitting in the Dory, which was at the time tied up alongside.

Since then, Dave had undergone the lion's share of mishaps and the sea seemed to be a magnet to his misfortunes. Various pieces of ship's equipment and clothing had finished up in there, all courtesy of Dave.

I didn't want to burst his bubble too soon, so I held back on explaining things to him. For someone who knew nothing, there was a lot to learn. And it was going to be much worse than that, for someone like Dave. I thought the best way was to teach him stuff as we went along.

We sat down, side by side on the wooden tool chest, surveying our domain, as I'd done so often before with Martin.

"They're big aren't they," he noted, pointing at the two engines. Then looking upwards he pointed at the two telegraphs. "I recognise them of course. Seen Al ring down the instructions from inside the wheelhouse."

I let him have a moment to take it all in. He must have been feeling nervous inside. I remembered feeling like an imposter myself, the day Al gave me a tour round, during my job interview. I'd come a long way in such a short space of time.

"The most important thing to remember, Dave, is to just be aware of all the moving parts. When the engines start up, don't go sticking your fingers in anything."

"Okay Byrney. Whatever you say." I could tell he was feeling apprehensive, so we talked about our childhoods. Dave was from Norwich, which explained a lot I thought. Not exactly a seafaring town. But Dave corrected me as the town centre actually had a working commercial port on the River Wensum.

'Oh well, Wensum, lose some', I thought.

Dave told me, he'd not had a happy relationship with his dad. "He never gave me a chance. If I couldn't answer one of his questions within a few seconds, he used to give me a thick ear."

By the end of our little chat, I'd learnt a lot about Dave - mostly about his past. And the more I heard, the more I felt sorry for him. I saw this as a chance to help Dave and I was determined to make him a success, if I could. In light of recent events, I needed something positive to feel good about too.

"Come on Dave," I said, standing up and walking over to the 'gubbings end' of the engine, where the complicated stuff was attached. "You'll soon get to like it down here. There's just the two of us, so don't worry about making any mistakes to begin with. No one's going to know about it." Spoken with my fingers crossed behind my back.

The journey west from Cap d'Ail to St. Tropez lasted just over four hours. For an new, old hand like myself, it was all very straightforward stuff and everything behaved as it should. The sea was relatively calm, so we'd had our portholes fully open the whole time. We kept a check on the engines and generator and I let Dave write up the details in the engine room log book. For four hours, at least, it was happy, plain sailing.

When the order came for 'Finished with Engines', I shook Dave's hand and said, "Well, what do you reckon, easy-peasey eh?"

"Not as bad as I thought it was going to be," replied Dave.

"Thanks pal. I'll tidy up in here. You'd better go and check with Gareth, in case we're both needed later to help with the Italians.

Back in my cabin, I'd a bit of a shock when I opened my door to find Magenta lying on her back, fully clothed on the top bunk. She turned over and stared pleasantly at me, brushing her hair to one side.

"Hope you don't mind. I just needed to get a little peace and quiet."

"Yer, that's fine," I replied, kicking off my yachty shoes.

"I see you've still got blue toes," she laughed.

I felt myself blush, but as the cramped cabin had very little natural light to illuminate my complexion, it went unnoticed. "I guess you've heard about the row I've had with Fi?"

"Don't worry, Byrney, she thinks a lot of you. Once she's over the shock of discovering you're a bank robber, I'm sure she'll be fine with it."

"Haha, nice one. You know how to cheer me up."

"Hey, you're not sulking are you?"

"Nah. I've just had a shit couple of days that's all."

"Hey, maybe we can slip ashore tonight if it's quiet. Have you ever been to St. Tropez? Maybe we can get you fixed up with a film star."

"I think I've got enough on my plate right now, thanks. But a couple of beers would do the trick."

Magenta stepped down from the top bunk and gave me a friendly peck on the lips. "That's more like it. See you later Romeo."

Gareth had taken the Dory to pick up the Italian film crew, from the quayside at St. Tropez marina.

I was standing in the galley, chatting with Dave and Magenta, when they came on board, all four of them: two blokes and two ladies. However, between them, they made enough noise to sink a battleship. I observed them venting their dramatic conversation, with an accompaniment of hand and arm signals.

Al greeted them with a glass of champagne and Fionn showed them to their quarters. They followed her like sheep. The lady who was last in line, looked like the star of the show. She glanced over her shoulder, fluttering her long, dark eyelashes at us, as she followed on behind, on her tip toes. She had the most curvaceous figure I'd ever seen. I never knew they made women like that.

"Put your eyeballs back inside your head, Byrney," quipped Magenta. "That's not one of your best looks."

Meanwhile, Gareth had returned to the marina at St. Tropez, to collect their bags of equipment. There was so much of it he had to make several trips, with Dave helping with the humping and dumping. Inevitably, by time it was all lugged aboard, there was nothing left of the evening for soaking up the nightlife in St. Tropez, at least not for the moment.

"This is going to be fun," said Al, in a laconic tone as he grabbed a cool bottle of beer from the fridge. "Out of the four of them, there's only one who can speak any English. I haven't a clue what their schedule is. I doubt they even know themselves, so we're going to have to play along by ear." He looked at Magenta and said, "Italian's one of your languages isn't it?"

"Yes, you know it is. Italian, French, Spanish and Portuguese of course. I'll speak to them in the morning. I can see this being a long seven days."

"Actually, it's only five days. We drop them off here again, around the middle of next week."

We looked at one another's tired faces and called it a night.

Fionn had her head down when I passed in front of her to wish her 'Goodnight', but she gave no reply. As I left I could hear Magenta explaining to Gareth how to say 'yes please' and 'no thank you' in Italian. It sounded nothing like, in Gareth's cockney'ese:

'seagrassy, nograssy'.

I could hear shouting coming from the direction of the aft deck. It was incredible how easily noise travelled, out at sea. I couldn't understand a word of what was being said. Then I remembered the Italians were on board. They'd started early this morning.

They were still performing long after breakfast had been cleared away. Their random shouting was very distracting, so I decided to take a peek at the action from the partially hidden gallery of the upper boat deck. As soon as I reached the top of the stairs from the back of the galley, I spotted Fionn and Magenta leaning over the wooden handrail. They had their backs to me and were looking over towards the open aft deck. I sauntered over and stopped at the opposite side to them. Down below, I could see a man and the curvy women. They were having a domestic. It looked like the sort of kitchen sink drama I was used to seeing back in England, on a Monday and Wednesday night, when mum took over our television to watch her favourite programme - Coronation Street.

The two actors below could easily have passed for a Latino twist on Elsie Tanner and Len Fairclough, although Granada TV would never had allowed Elsie to reveal so much bare flesh. And Len might have had a hairy chest, but he'd never, to my knowledge, worn a gold medallion, permed hairdo and a bronzed suntan; at least not in the confines of his builder's yard, back in Weatherfield. 'What a shame,' Mum would've said.

Magenta was now standing next to me, with a typed piece of paper, written in Italian.

"What's occurring then?" I asked, casually, trying to look over her shoulder to see if Fionn was looking this way at all.

"Quando il sole tramonta," She answered, with a perfect Italian accent, slowly raising her right hand for dramatic emphasis. "When the sun sets."

"Is that the name of the film?"

"Yes. It's a little corny, don't you think?"

As usual, Magenta was looking amazingly cool in her customary dark shades and plum coloured lipstick. She looked to me like she should've been the one being featured on celluloid and not this troublesome looking maiden stretched across the aft deck. The action was constantly interrupted, for longer periods than the camera was actually recording it, which must have been tedious and annoying.

"So what's the film supposed to be about?"

"I think it's about a holiday romance. But it's not very convincing. Neither of them look as though they are falling in love."

I noticed how the female star was dressed, well it was hard not to. What she wore didn't leave much to the imagination.

"The names of the actors, it says here," continued Magenta, holding up the piece of paper, "are Sylvia Fani and Lando Longo." She laughed. "Makes you wonder what kind of a film they're actually making."

Gareth was right after all, I thought. No one had ever heard of them.

"The guy doing the shouting is the one who can speak a little English. He's the director, Andrea Pisano."

"I couldn't imagine this going out on the BBC," I joked.

"Don't you get late night television in West Lancashire? Haven't you ever seen a drama called Nana on BBC2? Lots of scenes involving nudity and riding crops - very risqué."

I wasn't quite sure how to answer that. Fionn was the one who knew about horses. Although I'd never heard her mention she played that type of tally-ho.

"You're blushing again, Byrney."

"Yer, it's just the hot sun. Think I'll go and cool down in the shade of the engine room. I ought to be spending more time training up Dave."

Peace returned to the lazy afternoon. We were still at anchor, but the wind had moved the boat around so that our bow was facing into the harbour. Our guests had been ferried back to shore, together with several bags of equipment. This was a real shoestring film crew, but there was something quite fascinating about the whole filming process. The camera shots themselves were done very quickly. The director held the camera on his shoulder and moved from one angle to the next, controlling and orchestrating the two performers. The second lady, the directors assistant, was some kind of Girl Friday, checking everything from the light meter to Miss Fani's make up.

The evening on board was almost a rerun of the previous night, except when it came to wishing everyone goodnight, I overheard Gareth asking Magenta how to say 'Stop' in Italian and 'Leave me alone.'

At first light, I heard the Davit motor whining under a heavy load. Someone must be lowering the Dory into the sea.

Breakfast was disrupted again, by the familiar shouting coming from the aft deck.

"Come on Dave, bring your cup of coffee. Let's have a quick look at what the film crew are doing today."

When we reached the boat deck, Fionn and Magenta were stood in the same spot as yesterday too, but this time they were stood talking to Andrea. He was smiling and speaking in a very charming way. He was also trying to put an arm over Magenta's shoulder, but she was having none of it. Which made me smile. He didn't understand Magenta's 'look but don't touch' attitude. He switched his attentions to Fionn, working his charm and it appeared to pay off; he'd persuaded her to join in the action in one scene. He lead her down the staircase, through the salon and out onto the film set. I noticed too that Gareth was sat in the Dory about twenty yards beyond our stern. I looked over at Magenta. "What's going on?"

"Fionn's been asked to push Sylvia over the side."

"Really? Sounds a bit dangerous."

"I don't think they are actually going to do it. Probably cut the camera shot just before, and then switch to Sylvia floating on her back."

"This sounds like a laugh. I gotta see this," said Dave, enthusiastically.

When everyone was in position, Andrea counted down. Three, two, one, action. Fionn was holding a tray of drinks. She had her back to the camera and Sylvia began to stagger backwards, away from her partner, Lando. The director wasn't happy with the shot, so everyone was made to start over. He checked the drop again from the aft deck, which was about ten feet to the waterline.

"Three, two, one, action." This time when Sylvia staggered backwards, Fionn passed the tray to Lando and attempted to save Sylvia from falling overboard. After each take, the glasses on Fionn's tray had to be refilled. So by the tenth or eleventh take, Lando and Sylvia were getting quite merry.

On take thirteen, Sylvia accidentally lost her footing and disappeared backwards over the aft deck. Her muted cry was snuffed out by the loud splash, which confirmed she had landed safely. Everyone rushed to the side as Gareth steered the Dory alongside Sylvia's flailing arms.

Lando finished his lines in front of the camera. Presumably, lamenting the loss of his lover. Whilst all this was taking place, Gareth and Sylvia were having some kind of warm-hearted altercation in the Dory. Gareth was signalling to Andrea to get his attention.

"Yes, come. Bring back, please, now," he said through his loud hailer.

Sylvia wobbled up the side steps, looking like a drowned rat. Her wet hairdo matted with her war paint. She stepped straight into the arms of Girl Friday, who was stood in attendance with a dry bathrobe.

"I don't know why she bothered to wear a costume," said Dave. "You can see clean through it."

'Yer I noticed those too,' I thought to myself. "Come on Dave. We'd better get back to work."

So, at last, later that evening, I was able to see what all the fuss was about with Saint Tropez. We stopped off at the first restaurant we came upon - Chez Gerald. Having walked the length of the marina to get there, we'd already come far enough and time was of the essence. The immaculate yachts of all shapes and sizes, but mainly big ones, were moored together, line after line, mere glamourous toys to the rich and famous. It was all about showing off. The stinking rich liked to be seen on their exclusive, floating palaces surrounded by beauty that only a pile of money could buy. It was understandable why Al had decided to anchor offshore. And it was a pity he'd chosen to miss our soiree. He pointed out that he'd seen it all before, but the rest of us knew Al was also very careful with his own money. So he and Fionn had volunteered to stay on board, to look after our so-called film stars.

We were sat on hard, bamboo furniture on a shady terrace, watching the sun slip over the horizon and the tourists slide past the front of our table. Magenta was explaining the concept of the French 'Flâneur'. "There are those who prefer to promenade in front of the terrace as if it were an imaginary cat walk. They like to feel the gaze upon them. Then there are those, sat at the tables, who prefer to do the watching. But who is watching who? Really, it was just a game about posing." There was no answer to that, other than it was entertaining for a short time, I suppose. I noticed Magenta was wearing the same, elasticated blouse she'd worn that night when we ran down the street together from Rosie's; it made me smile again. Myself, I'd temporarily given up on fashion. It was always too warm to wear my favourite, black leather bomber jacket. Besides, most of the time I was in uniform and the only fashion accessory I needed was a decent t-shirt. I noticed most of the yacht goers were wearing look-a-like Bjorn Borg polo shirts by Fila: white, with thin red stripes and a blue collar, a real classic.

Gareth was telling jokes as usual: observational type stuff about which girls were wearing the skimpiest dresses, or the shortest hot pants. He was keeping a look out too, for Brigitte Bardot. There was a rumour she was in town as she lived close by. With Bardot, clothing was 'optional', according to Magenta.

"She's a proper actress," claimed Gareth, "Not like that Sylvia. She's a raving sex maniac. When I fished her out of the sea this morning and sat her down next to me, she kept trying to grab hold of my nob."

"It's the curse," I joked.

If Rosie's bar in Monaco was a homage to motor racing then Chez Gerald was the same to movies. Dotted around the walls inside the bar were framed black and white photographs of stars from the past. When I looked closely they all had one thing in common - they were all partnered by a wrinkly face, with a bow tie and a badly fitting wig. This must have been Gerald in his younger days. I recognised some of his clientele: Yul Bryner and David Niven, but mostly they were home grown French actors.

Magenta was rattling off all their names: Alain Delon, Serge Gainsbourg, with his wife, Jane Birkin and Gerard Depardieu.

"Who's your favourite?" I asked.

"Alain Delon. He's devilishly handsome, but he always plays the bad guy. This photo of him comes from the movie 'La Piscine'. It was filmed somewhere around here." Funnily enough, out of all the faces in the photos, his looked the coolest.

"Never heard of it. What's it about?"

"The usual French romance. Jealousy, betrayal and murder."

After an entertaining evening, we were back on board, once again lined up inside the long, narrow galley. I was watching Fionn, who was still toing and froing, doing the fetching and carrying for our noisy guests. We all heard Sylvia pipe up when Fionn handed them their latest round of drinks. "I want Gary. Where's Gary?"

Fionn returned, smiling at him. "I think she's sloshed again. You've made quite an impression on her, Gareth." Fionn was stood at the opposite end of the galley, still keeping her distance. I tried to acknowledge her with a smile, but she turned away and continued chatting with Gareth, who was looking decidedly worried.

As we retired to our bunks I heard Magenta giving Gareth more lessons in Italian: 'sono un uomo sposato.'

Around midnight, I was woken by someone knocking at my door. In my semi conscious slumber, I thought it was New Zealand Trev, but on the next round of banging, I realised the knocking was to the cabin door opposite.

"Gary, please let me in."

Gordon Bennett, it's Sylvia. How the hell had she got down here? Then she began humming a tune. I opened my door a fraction and peered through the gap. Sylvia's head was slumped against Gareth's door and she was trying to squeeze her words through the slit between the door and the frame.

"Gary, Gary. Do you know this song?" Her voice was slurring badly. "Let's spend the night together, now I need you more than ever..." Just then the door opened briskly and Sylvia almost fell into the room, before stepping back in a stunned silence. Facing her was Magenta.

"Will you go back to your own cabin," she said angrily. "Gareth is with me."

I closed my door quietly and slipped back under my cotton sheet. I was as stunned as Sylvia. They'd kept that quiet, between them.

The next day, everyone was creeping about like little mices. Filming had been cancelled for the day.

"Sylvia is feeling unwell, today. Perhaps she is well, tomorrow," announced Andrea.

Magenta came clean about sleeping in Gareth's cabin. She and Fionn had done a swap for the night with Gareth and Dave. So it all turned out to be quite innocent after all.

When it came to shooting the water skiing scenes the next day, Al was at the controls of the Dory. Gareth spent the day hiding inside the laundry room, refusing to show his face. "I've had enough of that Sylvia Fani. She can stick her fani up her arse, for all I care."

Dave's puzzled expression was a picture trying to figure that one out.

It was a relief to see the Italians climb down the side steps and into the Dory, back to St. Tropez. No one was more relieved than Gareth. He'd met his match with Sylvia. Full on, she was almost unstoppable.

I couldn't say I'd learnt much about the film making process either, just the fact that, if this was a taste of Italian films, then I hadn't missed much. And as for film stars, I hoped they weren't all as demanding as Sylvia Fani. But then again, who knows?

Later, in the quiet aftermath of a guest free afternoon, I found Magenta, on the boat deck, reading a book of French poems. She was still waiting for her big break. I told her she didn't need to pretend to be cool by acting. She looked the part in real life. I asked her if Fionn was showing any signs of forgiveness in my direction. If only she'd speak to me, even if it was just to say good morning. I felt truly miserable and helpless about being frozen out of her friendship.

Chapter Seven

True Colours

Captain Al, our hairy faced boss and guardian of our souls at sea, was holding court at the big breakfast table, out on the aft deck. He sat with his back to the sliding saloon doors as Fionn served up an English style cooked treat - scrambled eggs and bacon. "Luvlee!" announced Gareth, rubbing his eager hands together.

Prior to the arrival of the hot food, Al was explaining to Dave that we'd be sailing downhill later today. If there's one abiding memory that will linger with me, long after my days aboard the Liberty Angel are over, it's the scene of us all sat around the breakfast table listening to one of Al's anecdotes. Most of them were old seaman's wives tales, but hearing them became a routine, which no one wanted to miss. Gareth called it 'The Morning Chronicle'.

"That's impossible," protested Dave. "Everyone knows the sea is flat."

"Well, you're about to learn something new, Dave."

I had my head down, getting stuck in and splashing the brown sauce over my eggs, and wondering to myself what Al was going to say next.

"The Mediterranean has a natural current circulating around it." Al made a circle with his right hand. "The Med's practically sealed off, apart from the narrow opening across the straits of Gibraltar. Every day millions of gallons of sea water flow out into the North Atlantic and roughly the same amount flows back in, to replenish the loss." He turned to look at Dave. "With me so far?" Not waiting for a reply, he quickly continued his tale. "The current flows from west to east along the north coast of Africa, then turns northwards around Cyprus, eventually heading up the Ionian and Tyrrhenian Seas and finally down past the Balearics.

"Ooh," interrupted Gareth, pretending to shudder. "That Sylvia had hold of me by the Bally-airics."

"So," continued Al as he waited for some of us to stop laughing, "When we have a strong southerly wind blowing like today, it pushes against the surface of the sea and increases the height as it moves along. So later on, when we head south, we'll be sailing downhill." There was a moment's silence before Dave found an answer.

"What a load of old codswallop."

I realised Al had actually given Dave some food for thought, which meant in reality, it'd be playing on his mind for the next couple of days.

Magenta had taken the team minibus out to Nice airport to pick up our next bunch of paying guests who, according to Al, were members of the British aristocracy. "Might be a big tip at the end of the week, if we all make them feel welcome and give them a memorable time." Gareth and Dave were rubbing their hands and when Al mentioned we'd be stopping off in Corsica again, this produced a broad smile from Fionn. She had missed out on our last tour around the fourth largest isle in the Med, thanks to the lousy Americans.

Down in the silent engine room I was having trouble with getting Dave to understand the process of transferring fuel out of the main tank and into the day tank, which supplied fuel for the running of the engines and generator.

"Think of it like you're moving cows from one field to another. Picture the gates to each field. You have to open them to let the cows pass through. It's just the same with fuel, except we have wheel valves instead of gates. The valves are all tagged up. But if you forget which one to open, just follow the pipeline."

I showed him which valves to use and where the switches were for the transfer pump, red for stop, green for go. Think of the pump like it's the farmer and his dog, chasing the cows along. Dave took out his notebook and I helped him to draw up a plan to illustrate their positions. "What sort of dog is it?" he asked, pretending to wind me up.

"Okay, switch on the pump and keep your eye on the fuel gauge. When it gets to around three quarters full, switch off the pump."

"What happens if I forget to switch it off?"

"I've no idea. But there's probably an alarm in Al's wheelhouse and he comes down here with a hammer and hits you over the head with it," I laughed. "Just concentrate on the gauges Dave and you'll be fine."

I left Dave to it whilst I went to pick up a few bottles of water from the galley. As I stepped out from the gantry on to the poop deck, I bumped straight into Magenta who just going through her ritual of removing her hat and gloves and shaking down her hair.

"Sorry," I said innocently. "I'd no idea you were here."

She just smiled and shook her head all the more from side to side. "We must stop meeting like this," she teased.

Then, changing the subject before my face turned crimson, I asked her what were our aristocrats like?

"The usual kind. Eccentric and drunk."

"Sounds like our sort of people. Still, as long as they're happy eh?"

When I stepped into the galley I heard an unmistakeable voice coming from the salon and I feared I knew who it belonged to. "Surely not," I said to myself. I stuck my head around the corner into the passageway for a peep, but it was too late. We both recognised each other instantly.

"Well, if it isn't Rude Boy. What are you doing here?"

Oh no, Julie Nugent. So our big aristocrats are Lord and Lady Nugent from Cockerham Hall. I had to agree, it was 'rather a coincidence.'

"Have we met before?" enquired his Lordship as we shook hands.

"You probably won't remember me sir. I was a guest at Miss Julie's twenty-first birthday party." I saw the look of horror on his face. He'd obviously hoped the memory of the outcome of the party had been long forgotten, but Julie kindly reminded him.

"Remember dada? That was the night we rushed you off to Lancaster Royal Infirmary, to get your stomach pumped." This, his Lordship completely ignored and continued to quiz me, as a way of brushing aside his daughter's last comment.

"So, you're crewing down here in the south of France. What's the pay like, tolerable?"

"Dada, stop embarassing Byrney."

"Sorry sir, but I have to be getting back to work." I replied and for some reason, through sheer nervousness, I made a salute with my right arm and did a military style about turn.

I walked back to the engine room, cringing at my ludicrous escape from his Lordship. I was also having flashbacks about how my bubble had been burst before by Julie, when she'd made a sudden appearance that night at the Star pub, during my first date with Max.

"Friends of yours, The Nugents?" whispered Magenta. She must have heard and seen everything.

"I'll tell you later," I said quickly, still juggling with my thoughts.

Al was standing next to Dave in the engine room, when I returned.

"I've got some good news for us, chaps," he said. "We've got some reinforcements joining us at the end of the week, Kieron Woodcock. He's crewed with me before. Bloody good deckhand, very reliable and just the sort of help which Gareth could do with."

"Excellent. So what's the plan for today, Al?" I replied.

"Right Byrney, same as before, first stop Ajaccio. Think you'll be okay?"

"Yes, we're ready when you are." I looked at Dave, who nodded in agreement.

"I'll give the guests half an hour to settle in, then we'll cast off."

When Al disappeared, I noticed Dave was looking troubled.

"Anything wrong?"

"Looks like I'll be out of a job, when the new guy arrives." he bemoaned.

"Don't talk so daft. You're with me now and I reckon we're doing alright."

"One step at a time, eh?" he said chirpily, paraphrasing one of my routine instructions. "Does it feel like we're sailing down hill?"

I just laughed.

The favourable conditions lasted for just one more day.

I loved to wake up to unfamiliar sounds. All along the harbour front and the Jettee de Citella, a daily market was just setting up. Market people were totally inept at doing things quietly. Their stalls were constructed from aluminium poles, which had to be thrown down from the back of a lorry and dragged along the concrete pavement in order to sort them through and this could only be carried out by shouting instructions at one another. Listening to the racket gave me a reason to jump out of bed. A new day had already begun.

I climbed out onto the foredeck and was instantly aware of the floral, Corsican fragrance that floated in the air. It was such a sweet scent. The atmosphere appeared to be totally different from the street markets we'd seen on the boulevards in Paris. The whole island seemed much more Italian than French. Having spent the last five days with four of it's countrymen and women, I recognised the same dramatic mannerisms with the way the merchants set out their stalls. Perhaps it was something to do with the dramatic shape of the land. How it rose from sea level to over seven thousand feet, twice the size of the highest mountain in England. There was something impatient about their outbursts too, like they had to sell all their entire produce in one day. It must have been a disappointment to them to reload unsold stock back onto their vehicles at the end of the day.

I smiled at some of the strange vehicles that I saw being used to transport their goods - like the three-wheeler Piaggio Scooters, with their canvas canopied platforms. Someone had forgotten to tell the Corsicans that their small door-less cabs were built for just a single driver. Most appeared to be occupied by middle aged couples the size of Olympic shot putters. I couldn't imagine mum being lured into such a 'precarious looking thing'. She always had a high regard for her own safety, especially so when it involved doing anything with my dad.

The Jettee de Citella, lined with two rows of palm trees could have been a photofit for any town on the Cote d'Azur. The cloudless sky was the most intense blue I'd ever seen, which lead me to imagine the quality and variety of food on offer. It must be a chef's delight.

His Lordship and party had disembarked, immediately after breakfast, to soak up the ambience of the ancient, narrow streets and visit the local attractions, like the Napoleon Bonaparte museum. The midday sun would be beating down on them right now - mad dogs and Englishmen. Given the choice I would've been more inclined to join in with the locals: a long lunch, followed by an afternoon siesta.

From out on the boat deck I could hear familiar music, which was fast becoming the soundtrack to the summer - Fleetwood Mac's Rumours LP. Thinking it was Magenta, I went to investigate.

There was a female figure sunbathing. 'Oh bugger', I thought, it's Julie. It was too late to back away. I was very embarrassed at seeing her lying there topless. She held up the straps to her bikini top and turned over, asking me to rub some suntan cream into her shoulders.

"Sorry Julie, I really shouldn't be here." I said lamely.

"Well since you are here Byrney, it's fine with me. Here, rub it in." And she passed me the bottle.

"I can't, my hands are dirty."

"Well wipe them on your overalls. Really Byrney, it'll only take a minute."

I noticed she'd already tanned beautifully. "Just trying to get rid of these tiny strap marks," she sighed.

I quickly applied the sun cream and being so close to her, candidly observing her, I became aware of the amazing colour of her hair. "Do you mind if I ask you something?"

"Go ahead."

"Where did you get this fab coloured hair? I mean your mum is blond and your father's almost white."

"Well he wasn't to begin with," she laughed. "According to father, the red comes from our Irish roots. Did you know, ten per cent of the Irish population has red hair? That's the largest concentration by population anywhere in the world."

"Wow I'm impressed, but Nugent doesn't sound like an Irish name?"

"You're right, it's not. It originates from the time of William the Conqueror, when he brought his army over from Normandy. Many of the soldiers names just referred to the villages they came from, There were lots of villages called Nogent, hence Nugent."

"There, all done. Sorry I have to be going, but thanks for the history lesson. I enjoyed that."

"Perhaps I'll see you later. Are you allowed to go ashore?"

"Sometimes," I said.

A day later, I was stood inside the engine room with my feet plastered wide apart to maintain my balance, even when the sea was calm. Over the past few weeks, I'd got used to the feel of the ship rising up through the soles of my shoes; the tremors and vibrations of the screws rotating underneath the hull and the turn of the rudder, dragging the ship from side to side. Al coaxed the old vessel along gently and respectfully. So when I suddenly had to take a quick step forward to reposition my balance, it seemed strangely out of character. I knew instantly we were sharply changing course.

After a few minutes, Gareth rushed down the gantry steps. "Byrney!" He shouted. "We've got an emergency on our hands."

"What is it?" I asked. I could tell this wasn't one of his jokes.

"Al's just picked up a Mayday message. There's a ship about five miles away, it's the Liberty Princess."

"What sort of trouble?" My brain was suddenly in overdrive, trying to figure out what could be wrong.

"There's a fire in the engine room. Sounds like a bad one too. We should be in sight of her soon."

All three of us climbed the gantry to look out over the horizon. Up behind us Al was stood on the boat deck staring dead ahead through a pair of binoculars. We quickly moved around to the fore deck and immediately saw an ugly plume of black smoke.

"Shit, I hope everyone's ok." Realising Dave and me had to get back down in the engine room, I turned to Gareth and asked him to let us know when we were alongside. "You'd better get the Dory ready, in case we have to rush their crew to safety." Of all the places to run into trouble, they were around the halfway point, between Corsica and the French coast, almost fifty miles from the nearest stretch of land.

"It don't look too good," said Dave.

"No it bloody well doesn't."

I remembered as a child we had an incident of fire at home. Well, you couldn't really call it a fire. It was more like a freak accident. It occurred the evening before we were leaving to go on our summer holidays - camping in the Lake District. Dad was in the living room, changing the gas cannister on the portable table lamp. As he began to remove it, the residue gas, which remained in the old canister, began to escape and quite out of the blue, a spark shot out from our open fire and ignited the gas. The jet of roaring flames almost reached the ceiling. My dad yelled at mum, who ran in and began to panic, then immediately went to use the house phone in the hallway. I was sat on our stairs listening to mum scream at the 999 operator as dad began to kick the flaming cannister out of the living room, past mum through the hallway and out of the front door where it finally fizzled away, burning a patch of grass on our front lawn. What amazed me more than anything was how such a little flame had created so much drama.

I imagined the sort of drama, which must be taking place aboard the Liberty Princess right now - absolute blind panic, no doubt.

When we reached the stricken vessel, it was not a pretty sight. The Princess was listing badly, like she was already taking on water. Thick black smoke was billowing from every opening. This meant it was impossible for Al to bring us up close to the deck area. Gareth had lowered the Dory into the sea, but was arguing with Al. I rushed up onto the boat deck and Al turned to me and said, "Gareth's refusing to take the Dory across to the Princess."

"Why?" I asked.

"Ask him yer bloody self." I'd never seen Al lose his temper before. Gareth had overheard every word and before I could say anything he shouted, "That lot can screw themselves. I'm not putting my neck on the line to save them."

By now our guests had joined us and were asking if there was anything they could do to help.

"Any of you know anything about first aid," I asked.

Julie jumped forward and informed us she had just qualified as a veterinary surgeon. "I presume you have a first aid kit somewhere on board?"

"There's one in the wheelhouse, I'll go and fetch it right away," offered Al.

So it was agreed, I would take the Dory over with Julie and we'd remain in contact with Al through a pair of Walkie-talkie handsets. Magenta, who was also part of the discussion was persuaded to remain on board as we needed to save as much room as possible aboard the Dory in case we had to ferry everyone back here.

Gareth happily stepped aside to allow Julie and me to climb into the Dory. I was still shocked by his attitude. "Our friend Martin is over there and I thought you of all people, having known him the longest, would want to help him."

Al looked genuinely worried for us. I could tell at this moment he was having misgivings about letting us get close to the burning Princess. As yet we'd not seen or heard a cry for help from anyone on board. Radio contact had remained silent too, since their original SOS.

As we purposefully progressed towards the underside of the Princess, I noticed the tips of the starboard screw protruding out of the water. Gaining access onto the ship from this side of the hull was impossible. The handrail was far too high to reach. We'd no other option than to go around the stern to the smoky side of the ship. I looked at Julie. I couldn't tell what she was thinking from her expression of steely determination. I asked her if she was okay to proceed.

"Yes, we'd better take a quick look," she agreed.

The smoke didn't seem as thick or as dark once we reached the port side handrail. I secured the Dory with a couple of wraps of the line and a single knot. We both lifted ourselves up onto the aft deck and as soon as we reached the open saloon door we saw Dotty crouched over a wincing Eric Tyler.

"Thank god you've come," she sighed. "He's got some nasty burns to his arms and legs." Julie quickly moved in closer with her first aid kit. But judging from the rawness of his burnt flesh, I didn't think there was anything inside the little red box that would be of use. Eric had his eyes tightly closed.

"Where are the others?" I asked.

"Somewhere towards the fore deck. I haven't seen them since they brought Eric through."

I looked at Julie. "Do you think he can be moved? We'll need to get him into the Dory as soon as possible."

"We'll try," said the two girls.

I handed my walkie-talkie to Julie. "You'd better look after this."

Walking along the internal passageway was very disorientating, not just because of the acrid smoke, but because the ship was listing heavily and had begun to pitch forward too. The further I stepped inside, the warmer it became.

I soon came across Motty and Derek who were having a breather by the open door way. They were coughing violently and both of them looked shattered.

As I approached them I tried to make a joke of burning the sausages on their barbeque. Despite their obvious discomfort, they both looked delighted to see me. "Thank fuck you've come Byrney," said Derek hoarsely.

"What happened?" I asked flabbergasted.

"The fire started down in the engine room. It must have been the generator motor that overheated."

"Where's Martin?"

There was an exhausted pause from Derek's voice, then he said, "I think he's dead." followed by more coughing. After a moment, he continued, "Greg went down to find him and now he's disappeared as well."

"Show me how to get there."

"No, it's too bloody dangerous. The ships plates have warped in the heat and they're letting in seawater, which is why most of the fires have stopped burning."

"Look, we're talking about our friends here. We have to try to reach them at least."

"Ok," he said, "but only as far as the first deck. I'm not going below. The ship could sink at any moment."

"She feels stable enough right now. Come on, show me." We decided that Motty should help the girls get Eric on board the Dory, whilst I followed Derek towards the source of the heat.

At the engine room door, there were still remnants of smoke and steam billowing out of it. The taste of it instantly clung to the back of my throat and made me cough. My eyes began to sting and I was forced to look away for a few seconds.

"Don't go down there. It's suicide," he said.

I was trying to think fast. "Can you get me a rope, Derek? We can tie one end to the door and I'll take the other end down with me. I can use it to guide me."

After a couple of minutes, we'd managed to rig up a line. I asked Derek to wait at the top of the steps, but he was more concerned with rescuing valuables from the ship's safe.

I paused at the top of the gantry wondering if this was the right thing to do or not. Then I heard a faint cry from below. I stepped forward, keeping myself as low as I could. Everything I touched was red hot. I tore my wet t-shirt in two and wrapped the pieces around my hands. Luckily, I couldn't see any flames. Apart from a faint glow from a distant porthole, the natural light was almost totally eclipsed in the dense atmosphere. I remembered Al's words, 'like a steel coffin.'

"Hello?" I called out.

A faint groan replied. Please let it be Martin, but the voice was too weak to recognise. I felt my way further away from the foot of the steps accompanied by a lapping sound. My feet were now walking through seawater. I could just make out a pile of clothes, slumped against several lines of pipework. When I was close enough, I recognised his face - it was Greg. He was only half conscious.

"Where's Martin?" I asked.

Greg's eyes rolled into the back of his head and at the same moment there was a loud explosion just beyond us. The ship suddenly groaned too as it lurched over into a more acute angle, and stopped. On the decks above I could hear crockery spilling out and smashing into pieces.

"Gas bottles," moaned Greg. "They're exploding." The noise of the blast had obviously awoken him. I tried again.

"Where's Martin?"

"He's dead." I lifted Greg so that he could talk more freely. "There was nothing I could do for him. All the fire extinguishers were either faulty or empty." The thought made me feel sick. The taste of the fumes was beginning to overpower us both. The water level was now starting to rise rapidly and I knew we hadn't much time before the lower decks would be completely submerged. I fastened the end of the rope to Greg's waist and told him to follow me quickly. I hauled myself back along the line hoping Greg was following on behind.

When I reached the foot of the gantry steps, my lungs were nearly bursting. It took one almighty effort to climb them. I'd no idea where my strength came from. Having made it up onto the main deck, I was now crawling along the passageway when I felt a hand on my leg. It was Greg. He'd made it. When we reached the aft deck there was no sign of any of the others, or the Dory. The Princess was now listing alarmingly. One more explosion and it would all be over. We let ourselves slide down into the sea. I knew that, if anyone was coming back for us, we had to swim clear back around the stern. As we rounded the exposed propeller, which was now high above the waterline, I saw the Dory, heading our way with Motty at the wheel. It was a wonderful sight. I'd never been so glad to see anyone in all my life. I was hanging on to Greg as best I could.

"I think he's got concussion," I said to Motty, as he helped to drag his lifeless body inside.

When we came alongside the Liberty Angel, everyone was waiting for us. At the top of the steps, I fell forward, through sheer exhaustion. Fionn rushed forwards and put her arms around me.

"Thank god you're alive. I thought I'd never see you again, you crazy, loveable sod. Just look at the state of you." She held my head close to hers and stared straight into my eyes. "You're my hero. Thank you, for showing me your true colours."

The emotion of hearing Fionn's words and having her hug me so close to her, all got a bit too much for me and I began to cry, unashamedly.

When I opened my eyes again I saw that Julie was waiting in attendance to check I'd no physical injuries. The emotional ones had begun to heal themselves.

It's curious how you can sometimes look at people without realising what they are capable of. In my eyes Julie was every inch a hero too. She'd stepped forward with just a single thought of putting others first. It takes a special person to do that and I had so much respect for her.

Derek and Motty were equally full of praise for my actions. Derek described how I'd singlehandedly rescued Greg from the fire. But he also went on to say that these vintage yachts were 'bloody death traps' if their upkeep wasn't properly maintained. "The way those ship plates buckled," he ventured, "I wouldn't be at all surprised if they weren't corroded to half their original thickness."

His little speech was abruptly halted by a sickening, gurgling noise fifty yards away. It was the Liberty Princess sliding down beneath the waves. It was a haunting and terrifying sight, watching her disappear so easily, hastily and unceremoniously into the deep.

"Poor Martin," whispered Fionn sadly.

Immediately after the rescue, we'd headed back to our nearest port of call, Cannes, arriving there in the dead of night. There'd been a tune playing inside my head. The closing music that accompanied the end credits to the children's TV program Thunderbirds. Just humming it to myself. I'd no idea why. Perhaps it was a sort of homecoming. But more likely it was the dazzling effect upon my senses of all the flashing blue and orange lights.

At the quayside in Cannes we were met by two rescue service vehicles, which were waiting to taxi our walking wounded to hospital. Julie had done a remarkable job tending to Eric's injuries. His hands were badly burned and despite his best attempts to numb it with whisky, he was still in a great deal of pain. Greg was also helped into the back of the same ambulance. He'd taken a heavy blow to the head and he too was still suffering, from the after effects of concussion.

The Gendarmes wasted no time in taking statements from Al and Derek Watson. There were no incriminations at this stage. They were merely trawling through the motions of gathering evidence, whilst it was still fresh. The Liberty Princess was lost to the dark depths and the resulting chain of events had already begun to ripple to the surface. The thought of it left me feeling hollow and slightly afraid.

The seawater had found it's way through a rusted riveted seam between two plates. The joint ran vertically, mirroring the bow-shaped curve of the hull. My eyes widened as the hole too began to gape alarmingly, allowing the water to gush in, remorselessly. Martin quickly passed me his blue yachty shoes. Without thinking, I immediately tried to squash them into the gap to stem the flow of the incoming tide. So, Martin wasn't dead after all. The weight of pressure driving the water, forced it to fan out directly over the large electrical control panel. At the foot of the steel cabinet, the thick black cables had been severed. They now bore a life of their own, ducking and diving like angry serpents whose foul tempers, now wakened, made their mouths stretch, spitting blue white sparks. Sensing my fear they headed straight towards me. I was done for. I looked around for help, but Martin had gone. I was melded motionless. My arms, my legs, my whole body was paralysed with a cold cramp, completely soaked to the skin and knee deep in water. Only my thoughts could move. I was just one lick away from being turned into toast. Then I remembered that I had a neat trick up my sleeve. Even better than a 'Get Out Of Jail Free' card - I could just wake up, still with the same salty, acrid taste in my mouth.

By the next morning, the mood amongst the crew had lightened. There was still much to think about and discuss. So many things were happening in the background. After Al had spoken to old man Bailey in the early hours, he was informed that someone from the company's solicitors would be speaking to Martin's parents later that morning. By now an investigation by the insurance brokers was already under way, as well as the ones being carried out by the French maritime authorities.

Out of all the crew members from the Princess, only Derek remained on board with us. The others were either in hospital, or gratefully heading back home.

At the same time, we still had our guests on board. And although the wind had been taken out of their sails for more adventure, we still had to entertain and care for them. So it was agreed we'd gently slip along the short distance up the coast to Villefranche-sur-Mer.

The pretty coastal village with it's tiny splattering of bars and bistros looked immensely inviting and later that evening, his Lordship insisted on us all stepping on shore with them.

The meal that followed was one of the most intimate and thought provoking gatherings I'd ever taken part in. Even Gareth was unusually subdued, unable to inject us with any of his wry comments. Almost certainly, he was haunted by his own words. He hadn't lifted a finger to help in the rescue and I sensed the rest of us were, for the moment, giving him a wider berth. Each of us presently sat around the table had their own view about what had occurred. We'd all witnessed it. The sinking had left its mark on us all and its scars ran to varying depths, depending on how closely the tragedy was felt. From what I can remember, we all got pretty drunk attempting to escape its horrors.

Chapter Eight

Last Days

In the remaining days of their charter, Julie spent an increasingly amount of time in our company, even on occasion choosing to dine with us in the galley. No one protested. In light of recent events, Al allowed us to relax the normal 'master and servant' relationship with our paying guests.

With Julie hanging around us most of the time, I had to explain to Magenta and Fionn how our paths had crossed before, at the Star Inn and at Julie's country home, Cockerham Hall.

"So, she knew our Max very well too?" enquired Fionn.

"Yer, actually she'd known Max since their school days."

As the conversations moved back and forth between Julie, Fionn and myself, talking about Max was drawing the three of us into some kind of a curious web. Each of us had known Max in our own way: three points of view, three separate pieces, which just might uncover a truth. I was hoping I could pool our knowledge and work out the real reason why Max had committed suicide.

Fionn spoke about Max as a colleague at the Friary. To her, Max was someone who always seemed so sure of herself. "She was so composed," she said. "No matter how busy it got in the café, she never got into a flap like some of us did. She was always 'head girl', a bit like Magenta in that way. But you knew her intimately Byrney, after all she was your girlfriend for quite a while."

I sensed Fionn was handing the baton over to me.

"Yer, there were definitely two sides to Max's personality," I said, remembering last summer and trying not to blush. I wasn't going to betray any of our secrets. In my mind's eye, I still had that wonderful picture of Max, lying naked on the straw covered floor of the old mill on Weavers Lane. Her soft, warm body illuminated in the rays of the morning sunshine. In all the long days we'd spent together, she was always the one 'showing me the way'. But there was also an inner darkness about her that I never fully understood. It was obviously something deeply personal, which she kept buried deep inside.

"I think maybe it had something to do with her sister." Right now I wished I'd taken a closer look at the diary I'd found inside Max's doll. The only thing I'd learnt so far from it was her name - Kate Reid.

"I never knew she had a sister," said Fionn.

Up until this point in our conversation, Julie hadn't uttered a word. She listened intently, sipping her Martini and occasionally breaking out into an instantaneous laugh, or just smiling in agreement at our reminiscences.

"It's true Max did have an older sister, although I never knew Max then. She died when Max was only six years old."

"How awful," said Fionn. "Do you know how it happened?"

Julie began by telling us how she first became friends with Max. "Max's mum and my father both knew each other from their Cambridge days. Max's father had been at Cambridge too, but I can't ever recall Da'da ever saying he was part of their troop, perhaps because he was a northerner. You know how those Yorkshire types are keen to let the rest of the world know they have the best this or that." I knew exactly what she meant. My Uncle Ray always prided himself on being a Skiptoner, 'man and boy'. And then there were the endless arguments with dad about cricket, but it was all just light-hearted banter really.

"Max was six or maybe seven years old when she and her mum moved to West Lancashire. We went to the same boarding school together in Lancaster. I think my father helped to pull a few strings to get her in. I was a year above her, but Max was very physical. She loved hockey and netball. And it didn't take long for us to bond, playing in the same teams together. Being good at sports was our way of rebelling. You can bet your bottom dollar, if anything went missing, Max was usually behind it." Fionn and I both looked at each other knowingly, which Julie saw and misinterpreted. "No, she wasn't a thief," continued Julie in Max's defence. "Max just took things for devilment, but, on the whole, she was a lonely girl. Apart from me, she hadn't anyone she was close to, not even her parents. I don't ever remember her mum visiting her. She was often away, working somewhere on one of her design projects. But her father used to turn up out of the blue. I always found him to be a charmer, but I could tell Max hated him. He was always trying to please her, but she never allowed him near her. He used to take us out to the seaside, buy us ice creams, spoil us rotten really. Then, all of a sudden, he stopped coming, I'd no idea why."

Just then, Gareth and Dave both appeared on the boat deck.

"So this is where you're hiding," said Gareth, sniggering. "Sorry to break up the party, but Lord Nugent wants to learn how to water-ski." Gareth's announcement immediately set Julie off, guffawing. "Now this I have to see," she screamed with delight.

"We're just going to drop the Dory down. Give us a hand, Byrney."

"We'll catch up later," said Julie as she and Fionn descended into the salon whilst Dave and I removed the covers from our speedboat.

"She's a right laugh, that Julie," said Dave, as soon as the girls disappeared below. "You'd never guess she's related to the Queen." I looked at him in amazement, wondering where or from whom he'd got that from. 'He's priceless,' I thought.

Our week with 'The Nugents' was coming to an end and I'd still not had the chance to catch up on my chat with Julie. Perhaps there was something specific about Max's past that would explain why she'd killed herself. Since that awful day I'd been carrying a sack full of guilt around with me and I was still hoping to find a reason for Max's suicide other than my running out on her. Immediately after her death, I'd tried to shift the blame onto her mum, but since I'd now learnt Max had an older sister, who'd also died, maybe there was some hidden genetic fault at the heart of it.

On their final evening aboard, after their Lordships had dined on the aft deck, under a glorious Mediterranean sunset, Julie came looking for me in the galley and asked if there was somewhere private where we could talk.

In the stale silence of the engine room, Julie once again began talking about her days in the dormitories with Max. But there was still no clue as to why Max could be suddenly so withdrawn and tormented. I sensed Julie was holding back on something.

"Julie, you mentioned before that Max's dad suddenly stopped visiting. Was this something to do with Max's sister?"

For once Julie looked deadly serious. "Max asked me never to repeat this, but there doesn't seem to be any point in not telling you now."

"Telling me what?"

"Well, despite the fact Kate had taken an overdose, Max suspected her father had killed Kate." Julie's words hit me like a bombshell.

"What made Max think her father did it?" I was still trying to make all the pieces fit together.

"Max was the one who found Kate. Kate was in their parents' bedroom, lying on their parents' bed, wearing her mum's clothes."

"Didn't the Police suspect him?"

According to Max, she said that by the time the Police arrived at their house, Kate had been moved to her own bed and was in her own clothes. Max couldn't explain it. She even thought she might have dreamt it. Either way, she was too traumatised to say anything to the Police. Besides, not long after, her parents separated, and Max and her mum came to live on our estate for a brief time. Da'da lent them the lodge house. Looking back, Max must have felt very vulnerable, knowing her parents had tried to," Julie paused for a second. "Well, not cover up Kate's suicide, but they certainly tried to normalise how it looked. You have to admit there is something odd about that."

'God, poor Max,' I thought. I knew in part how she must have felt, living with that knowledge. I too was still haunted by Max's suicide. I turned to Julie and asked her if she thought I was in any way to blame for what she did, the day of Eve's funeral. Julie held my hand and squeezed it firmly. "Don't be so bloody daft. Max did what she did that day because of her childhood. Guard your demons, Byrney. Don't go poking them with your guilt. No good ever comes of dwelling on the past."

When the morning came and 'The Nugents' departed, I was actually sorry to see then go. Al and the rest of the crew, on the other hand, were highly delighted. Thanks to the generous tip left by his Lordship. At their final farewell, Julie suggested we should meet up back home, at the end of the season, one Friday night at The Star Inn.

"I'm there most weeks," she shouted as she waved goodbye. Fionn was standing by my side. "You're not going to, are you?" she asked.

"Probably not."

The following morning, we were once again back in our usual mooring, in Cap d'Ail marina, breakfasting in the warm sunshine. For once, Al was absent. Around the table, our crew now consisted of an additional permanent member, Derek Watson, formerly of the Liberty Princess. To Dave's delight, the elusive Kieron Woodcock, who'd had been earmarked to join our crew, had become, as Al put it, 'persona non grata' since the sinking. So, for the time being, Dave's presence aboard looked set to be permanent.

Amongst those present, a strange conversation popped up, about seagulls. Derek was explaining how to make them explode in mid air. It was the typical sort of gruesome tale, which normally coincided with us all eating.

"What you do, is you get hold of some bicarb of soda, wrap it in a piece of paper and throw it up to the seagulls when they're following the ship. When the bicarb digests in their stomachs, boom." I looked at Dave's reaction. For once, he was stumped for a reply. At least no comment was an improvement for dear old Dave.

When Al eventually sauntered up to our table, he didn't look his usual, chipper self.

"Anything wrong Skip?" Asked Derek.

There certainly was. Al raked back his chair and stood up. We all immediately fell silent.

"Listen up everyone. I've got some bad news. I've just got off the phone to head office and it appears that Liberty Yachts are currently under investigation and its current fleet of yachts including the Liberty Angel have been handed a movement ban until further notice. So, we're stuck in Cap d'Ail for the time being." We all looked at one another in silence, not yet knowing if this was a good thing or a bad thing.

"I presume this has something to do with the sinking of the Princess?" replied Derek.

"What do you think?" confirmed Al, in an irritated tone.

"I told Eric not to cut corners. That we'd all pay for it one day." continued Derek to no one in particular.

Al held up his arm to quell the murmurings. "It is, what it is." Which didn't make any of us feel any better. "Unfortunately," continued Al, "old man Bailey can only guarantee your wages for the next two weeks. And if we're still tied up after that, well, you might want to think about your futures."

I looked at Fionn and we both shook our heads slowly in disbelief. Was this the end of our adventure?

An hour later the majority of the crew, with two exceptions, held an unofficial meeting in the engine room, to discuss the depressing news. Gareth was the least happy amongst us.

"It's that bloody Derek's fault," he moaned.

"How do you work that out?" I replied.

"I tell you, he's a bloody Jonah that's what. I knew no good would come of having any of the Princess lot on board." Some of us just laughed discouragingly.

"Don't be bloody paranoid. If that's the best you can come up with, I'm off back to work," replied Magenta.

"It's alright for you, we all know you're Al's pet." The rest of us looked at Magenta, thinking she'd let Gareth have it, but she just carried on up the stairs. Her future was never in doubt, not because of Al, but because she was just so damn cool, I thought, cool and talented.

As the meeting dispersed Fionn grabbed my arm and passed me an envelope.

"What's this, Fi?"

"Open it; it's to both of us; I received it yesterday."

I stared at the card. It was a wedding invitation to Vicky and Kevin's forthcoming marriage. I'd completely forgotten they'd got engaged last year. Crowston and the Friary, it all seemed so long ago in the past. Then I noticed the date - next Saturday, a week from today.

"Why don't we go?" suggested Fionn. "There's nothing happening here that's going to spoil. Besides, I love weddings and as they're both friends of ours, I wouldn't want to miss this for anything."

"You're right. Let's go and see Al."

Weirdly, once we'd made up our minds to go back to England for a week or two, everything clicked into place, without a hitch.

That evening, the entire crew of the Liberty Angel were camped together, inside Rosie's bar for the last time. Some of us were drowning our sorrows, whilst others had already moved on with their own thoughts for the future. It looked to me like only Al and Magenta had a sense of permanence about them.

Magenta was quizzing me about the upcoming wedding. Who was Vicky and how handsome was Kevin? "I'll give it six months," she cruelly joked. Magenta of course was dead against tying the knot. There was no way she was going to honour and obey any man. I'd not been able to make any impression on her either. We'd had some great times together. We'd even shared a bed, albeit for just a few minutes. I smiled to myself at the thought of me falling asleep, instead of putting my arms around her. I used to think she was giving me the 'come on', but whenever I tried to get close, then the more she sidestepped the issue. I imagined putting my arm around her here right this minute. How would she react? She'd probably say something like, "Byrney, if you don't remove your arm, I'll break it for you."

"Cheer up, what are you looking so glum about?" she asked, handing me another bottle of seize, soixante-quatre.

"I was just thinking how I don't seem to have a long lasting relationship with a girl," I confided.

"Maybe you're just looking in all the wrong places."

"How do you mean?"

She didn't reply. She just winked at me and stared across at Fionn.

The next day, Magenta dropped Fionn and myself at the railway station in Nice. According to our tickets, we'd arrive in Paris at seven p.m this Sunday evening. Then we had the choice of spending the night there, or catching the night train back to London.

Before we left, Al had taken us both to one side. He was keen to emphasise we were both still part of his plans.

"Keep this to yourselves," he said. "But once we're allowed to sail again, there's a strong chance we'll be taking over the winter charters that had been scheduled for the Princess.

"What winter cruises?" Asked Fionn.

"The Caribbean," whispered Al, cagily. "Jamaica, Antigua, but it's hush, hush."

"Mum's the word," whispered Fionn excitedly.

I shook hands with Al and gave him a list of all the faulty fire extinguishers on board. "Three out of the four in the engine room are practically empty," I said. Which didn't exactly fill me with confidence about a possible two thousand mile voyage across the North Atlantic.

"Thanks Byrney," replied Al. "Like I said, we've got to pass a safety inspection before we're allowed to sail again. I'll make sure these are all checked and refilled."

"And the gland seals on the main shafts? Do you think they'll make it to the Caribbean?"

"All in hand Byrney. I've already asked for a quote from the dry dock in Livorno, Italy."

"That's good. Sorry to be a bit of a moaner, but after what happened to the Princess it's left me with the jitters."

Al laughed. "You'll be fine, don't worry. Enjoy your wedding and I'll see you both back here in ten days time."

Magenta had stopped the minibus right in front of the main entrance at Nice station. We grabbed our bags and thanked her for the lift. I watched Fionn sharing a warm hug with her. As cabin companions, they'd become very close over the past few months. When Fionn pulled away and straightened the hem of her skirt, Magenta looked at me and asked, "well, don't I get a hug from you Byrney?"

I wasn't about to refuse. She gestured with her hands for me to step forwards. "You look like you need some time out, take a couple of weeks off."

"Yer, I guess."

She gave me a passionate squeeze then dropped her arms by her side. Then she removed her dark shades and stared straight into my eyes. "You're not coming back, are you?" She'd been reading my thoughts. Whilst her mind was off guard, I gave her a peck on her plum coloured lips.

"We'll see Juliet, we'll see."

The sinking of the Princess had made a difference to how I felt about being at sea. It had taken a lot of the shine off my adventure. After Martin's death I no longer felt invincible. I was hoping this feeling would pass during my break back in England, but knowing now that Magenta doubted my commitment, led me to believe that Al and the others might also have their doubts about me. And in a strange way it made it easier for me to walk away.

The first thing we did when we arrived at Paris, Gare de l'Est was to walk the short distance to the Gare du Nord and check the train times for the night ferry. It was due to leave in exactly thirty minutes. Fionn quickly came to the same conclusion as me. As we were both on our way back, there didn't seem to be any reason to delay our arrival back home. In fact, having spent almost nine months away, we were both now looking forward to seeing our families again.

Whilst we waited, I went along to the station bureau de change. I still had most of the Spanish Peseta's in the bag, which I'd originally brought out with me. The French Francs however had all been spent a long time ago. The smart, uniformed lady behind the cash desk viewed me suspiciously, as she counted out the crinkled up notes. Then she asked if I would like Sterling.

"Oui, s'il vous plait."

As this was possibly our last journey together, I wanted it to be a nice time for Fionn to look back on. Although I still hadn't made up my mind about whether I was going back to the Liberty Angel and I wasn't going to rush into making a wrong decision. And so, for the time being, I said nothing about it to Fionn.

Once we were aboard the night ferry train to London, we found an empty compartment. We stored our stuff away and went to find the buffet car. We both felt like old hands. How we'd changed since our journey down here. We were no longer nervous, afraid of getting lost, nor afraid of the language.

"Voulez vous un boisson?" I ventured.

"Oui mon cherie," replied Fionn fondly.

"I'll choose something for us both."

When I returned to our little table I was carrying half a bottle of champagne and two glasses, "Surprise."

"I thought we were supposed to be saving money by taking the train instead of flying?"

"Well, we're only young once. Let's toast the health of all our friends we've left behind."

Our conversation continued in a nostalgic vein as we recalled stories from the past nine months.

"It's a shame Anna decided to stay in America," lamented Fionn. "I thought you were both really into one another."

"So did I, but there was always something which didn't quite sit right between us. I think it just boiled down to the fact she was French and I was English. Our two cultures are miles apart, but I have to admit, I'm becoming more in tune to the French way of life."

"Oh yes, you're right. I love it. The gorgeous food, the clear blue skies and the places we've seen have been unbelievable, not like anything back home, that's for sure."

We were rattling away to one another, completely oblivious to our surroundings. The rhythm of the train and the bubbles from the champagne were rolling an enchanted spell over us. Beyond the compartment window, the night sky descended and darkened deeper into the blurred landscape that only occasionally revealed distant lights of occupation, slumbering in the silence.

We were both drowsily reading in our bunks. The other two berths opposite were still untaken. When the words began to shift on our pages we rested our eyes. And turning out the lights we finished chatting to one another in the dark about our imminent homecomings.

"So your parents have moved to Skipton, that's such a shame. It's going to make it more awkward for you to get across to West Lancashire."

"True, but it's not too bad, just two buses, Skipton direct to Preston, from there up to Cayburn. But you're right, it won't be the same. I'm going to have to learn to drive. Night Fi."

"Goodnight Byrney."

At four o'clock the following afternoon, we'd reached our destination - Preston Railway Station. We trundled up the high street together, dragging our tired bodies in the direction of the central bus station. There were still plenty of late shoppers, barging past us with bulging shopping bags. We paused occasionally at some of the more interesting shop windows. Some new shops had appeared too, like the small independent clothing shop called Alien, where five youths were gathered outside. They all looked quite alien too in their tall spikey hair do's, wearing black leather biker jackets and ripped jeans, both heavily decorated with chrome chains, studs and safety pins. As we passed the open door, a blast of punk rock music belched out at us. As we continued up the busy street, I realised I would have to buy some decent clobber for the wedding, next weekend.

At the bus terminal, we checked the big notice board to see which stands we needed to be at. Fionn's timetable to Lancaster was much more populated than the one I needed for Skipton. Hence I had one hour to wait, whilst Fionn's bus was already taking on passengers.

"So I'm still okay to come and stay at yours the night before?" I asked.

"Yes, I've already said so three times."

"Then I guess this is where we go our separate ways." I said stepping forwards to give her a hug. "I'm really looking forward to the wedding and meeting up with everyone again."

Fionn stood there quietly, not yet wanting to join her queue, which had all but disappeared. I looked at Fionn's eyes. They were big and round and looked to be starting to glaze over. "You know, it's going to feel strange us not being together," she said. " You know, not bumping into one another on an hourly basis and sharing the same laughs."

I was stumped for words. What she'd just said was absolutely true. I'd not really thought about it like that, but I too felt the same bond between us. I watched her disappear inside and take up a seat by the window. She smiled at me and blew me a kiss. I placed a kiss for her in my hand and stuck it to her window and waved goodbye.

Chapter Nine

Retribution

Whilst I was waiting for the bus to Skipton, I found a public telephone box and gave my parents a call to let them know what time I'd be arriving. According to mum, it was only a short walk from Skipton Bus depot to Nana's house. We used to visit her regularly over the past two or three years, especially after grandpa had died. Nana was a capable and independent woman, not someone you would typically call old aged, but according to mum since the turn of this year, her health had begun to decline sharply. I was wondering how she felt about having three house guests, which was about to be four. When I spoke to mum she sounded flustered, like she hadn't been expecting me home so soon. Charming, I thought as I put down the receiver. One minute she doesn't want me to leave; now she doesn't want me to come back. Still, I guess they must be feeling the strain too. Mum and dad were still house hunting and as yet their search had been fruitless.

The bus journey in the early evening summer sunshine was very picturesque, once we'd escaped the urban sprawl of Preston, I'd forgotten just how lusciously green our trees and pastures were. The bus ride took in some wonderful rural scenes, along the Ribble valley from Preston Brook, past Whalley and on towards Gisburn, against the rugged backdrop of the Pennine hills. As the bus crossed over the county border, I felt the temperature drop a few degrees and the sky filled with grey clouds. With my feet back on the pavement, I was reminded too of the clinginess of cold damp air. Still, at least the brisk walk up to Nana's would warm me up.

The small white picket fence, with a border of red and white roses, soon came into view. It was very comforting to find it looked as it had done for as long as I could remember - 24 Duckett Street. Everyone was present inside to greet me, except our Anthony. He was out with a girl.

"Our Anthony's got a girlfriend?"

"Yes, he brought her here last week," informed Mum. "Such a funny little thing with short hair. At first I thought it was a boy," she laughed.

I opened my shoulder bag and handed out my presents from the duty free shop. I'd forgotten to buy anything for Nana, so I'd picked out some flowers from a stall on Skipton Market. They all seemed very pleased with their gifts: cigars for dad, perfume for mum and a pocket radio was waiting for Anthony.

"Sorry Mark, but there's been a slight change of plan," announced Mum. I sensed there was a slight atmosphere since I'd stepped over the 'unwelcome' mat at the front door.

"There's no spare bed for you, so you're going to have to stay across town at your Uncle Ray's."

"I don't mind kipping on the couch," I suggested.

"Well I do," replied Mum. "Sorry, but I'm not going to start creeping around you every morning when I'm trying to get ready for work. It's already decided. Your Uncle Ray will look after you."

"Okay then, I'll buzz off in a bit. Any chance of something to eat first, I'm starving."

"Yes love. Your dad's about to go to the chippy at the end of the street."

"Mmm lovely."

Whilst I waited for our newspaper wrapped dinner to arrive, I went to find my stuff from our mobile home. There were four boxes, labelled 'Mark's Bedroom', in a large pile, stacked up inside the garage. I opened them all up, to inspect what I'd left behind: my crash helmet, my vinyl records; of which I could tell some were missing, posters, school books, shoes and clothes and at the bottom of the last box, the item I'd been searching for - Kate Ried's diary.

Dinner was consumed on the sofa, watching an episode of Coronation Street. We were 'shushed' by mum until the adverts came on. Then we were allowed to talk, but the meal was marred, by niggling, bickering between mum and dad. They usually fell out where I was concerned. Mum was ever anxious to know that I was settled down doing a proper job. "So have you decided to reapply for the Royal Air Force?"

"I'm not sure."

"Leave our Mark to decide for himself," said Dad, sticking up for me. "He's not done a bad job of it so far."

"That's right, say the exact opposite to me!" shouted Mum.

The tension of several generations living under the same roof was taking its toll on their relationship. Then our Anthony rolled in late, accompanied by a waft of cheap cigarettes. He was obviously still gadding about on his chopper bicycle and he'd a red face to prove it. But other than that I hardly recognised him. He'd grown at least six inches taller and his robust figure had become stretched and lean. It didn't surprise me now to know he'd got a girlfriend.

After the meal, there was just enough time for him to play me a couple of his latest vinyl forty fives. I also noticed he'd added some of my records to his collection - 'well as long as you look after them. Make sure you keep them in the correct sleeves'. The song I really liked was the new one by a band called The Jam - In The City. It sounded fresh and new and full of energy, and had just the right mix of teenage angst and attitude. 'You had to be young and this was our time'.

The ambience at Uncle Ray's was the exact opposite to the one I'd left behind at Nana's - relaxed, organised chaos. And what wonderful chaos it was too.

Ray still looked like the mad professor with his uncombed, grey thatch, sprouting out like an electrified ball of wire wool. He was wearing a herringbone tweed waistcoat, which could have almost passed for trendy had it been worn with a grandad shirt and a pair of blue jeans. Instead, his baggy velvet pants had a unique shape all of their own - a slept in look with worn and threadbare knees. The same could be said for Ray's household furnishings too.

"Well if it isn't Marco Polo? Come in, come in, sit yourself down, I've been expecting you."

Once again, I was impressed by the grand proportions of the rooms at Mount Pleasant Villas on Gargrave Road. They were a stark contrast to the closetness of 24 Duckett Street. It was less than a mile and a half away, but culturally half a century in advance. I loved being surrounded by his books and magazines, even if a good proportion of them were still stored inside various tea chests. But these too didn't look out of place amongst the bulkily occupied coat pegs in the long tiled hallway, overflowing with coats, hats and fishing rods.

"I was just about to open a bottle of red. Do you fancy a glass? No doubt you'll be a connoisseur, having spent the best part of a year on the continent."

"Yer I've had a few interesting bottles," I boasted. "For my seventeenth birthday I had a Margaux Nineteen-sixty."

"Oh, you lucky bugger. What was that like?"

"Yer, okay. I only remember getting drunk and going outside to stare up at the stars."

"Gosh, that good eh? Well I don't have anything as formidable as a Margaux, but this bottle of Saint Emillion from last year is rather splendid."

The cork made a delicious popping sound as he held the bottle between his legs to extract it. That was a sound no one could possibly tire of hearing, I thought, that and the first few glug, glug, glugs as Ray poured half the bottle into two large glasses.

"Sante," he said.

"Et votre sante aussi, mon oncle." I replied instinctively.

"So tell me, what have you been up to. I'm dying to hear about all your adventures."

Half way through the second bottle of wine I was just about done in. I'm not sure if Uncle Ray believed half of what I'd been saying about my time in Nice, Toulouse and the Pyrenees. I broke off at the point where I'd managed to reunite Eve and Paul's ashes, never once referring to the stolen loot. It had been a long old couple of days since leaving Cap d'Ail and as the grandfather clock down in the hallway struck midnight, I timbered, fully clothed, onto Uncle Ray's spare bed.

The next morning, I was awakened by a dawn chorus. It took me a few seconds to realise where I was. I followed the patterned wallpaper around to the curtains, which were billowing gently in a fragrant breeze, by the partially opened sash window. The sun highlighted the shadows of the narrow glazing bars. Then, as my groggy, conscious state refocused I remembered more: waking in the night feeling uncomfortable and changing into my pyjamas and sliding under the feathery eiderdown.

I nipped down the steep staircase and raided a packet of Jaffa cakes from the Kitchen - it was only seven a.m. and the rest of the house was still snoozing. Returning to my springy bed, I grabbed my bag and found what I was looking for inside the zipped compartment - my pocket radio and Kate's diary. I opened up the first page as I munched away, listening to Noel Edmonds breakfast show on Radio One.

The neat handwriting appeared on the opening page, which I'd seen before. This diary belongs to Kate Ried, 2 Wood End, Farley-in-Craven. I'd never heard of Farley, but maybe it wasn't all that far away. I'd noticed a road sign for Thornton-in-Craven, near Broughton Hall on my bus journey yesterday.

The diary began with observations and destinations: trips to the park with dad to look at the aviary, playing on the swings with her little sister, Max. However, I soon became aware that what was written on the pages that followed were no ordinary, childhood recollections. The author wrote about her mum's long and frequent absences. She was worried about being alone with her dad. I got a sense of her anxiety – her mum was working away again. Further into the diary, she wrote in more detail. *Dad came to my bedroom again last night.* She wrote this on three occasions in the same week. On the third entry she added, *'he really hurt me. I wish mum was home.'* She also wrote about being lonely at school, about having no close friends, no one to share with about what was happening at home. She didn't mention about the park or the swings anymore, only that her dad was always telling lies to her mum.

In August, she began senior school, but instead of finding a friend, she found that now she was the focus of bullying: *'Everyone in my class picks on me because I live out in a backward village. They call me one of the Clampits. They pull my hair and empty everything out of my satchel.'*

Reading these sad pages, I was also aware that this story wouldn't end well, particularly as the pages from October onwards were all blank. In the second week of September came half term, but there was no holiday from the torture she faced at home. Instead of them going away as a family, her mum was away by herself again, working. Kate's focus now seemed to be on protecting her younger sister, Max.

She wrote *'if I don't do what daddy says, he says he will start to do the same to Max as he does to me. I cry a lot, which only makes dad more angry. I know I have to hold out until mum gets home. Dad won't dare touch Max while she's around. Dad is with us all day. It's worse when it's raining because we can't play outside. He watches me all the time. I hate it when he wants to bath us both'.*

September 22nd; Mum is home tomorrow. I know she won't believe anything I say. Dad always has a lie ready. He smiles and everyone believes him. I hate him.

September 23rd; last night was the worst. I've had to change my bed-sheets to hide the blood. Please come home mum, please look after Max'.

'My god, the poor kid,' I thought. Her father was a real, evil bastard. This was the last entry, the last sad lines written by Kate. I knew I had to try and fill in the rest of the story, or at least try to confirm what Julie Nugent had told me, about how Kate died. If it had happened sometime after September 23rd 1963, then more than likely it would have been reported in the local newspaper. But where was Farley, I wondered. Perhaps Uncle Ray might know something.

A little later that morning, at the breakfast table, I just came straight out with my question. I asked if Uncle Ray knew of a place called Farley-in-Craven.

"Yes, it's about six miles out of Skipton on the other side of the heath. Bit of a wild and lonely place, even in June," he laughed. "But I wouldn't waste my time going there. There's nothing much to see, just a few houses and an old church. Half of them are either derelict or empty."

He carried on eating, but I wasn't about to be put off. "Do you still get a copy of the Craven Times?" I asked.

" I do - have done for over twenty years. But these days, like a lot of things that have been around a while, you get less of it and it costs more money. It's the way of the world," he continued, dreamily. "I've got a tea chest full of old copies. I can't bring myself to throw them out. That's our local history."

"Don't suppose you have any from 1963," I asked, tentatively.

"You up to something lad?" He viewed me over the rim of his glasses and took another bite of toast.

"Not really, just a bit of research, that's all."

Uncle Ray looked down at his toast again and coated it with an even thicker layer of silver shred, then took another bite.

"That's better. You can't beat a bit of toast on your marmalade," he smiled. "I'll dig all the sixty-three's out for you before I leave. I know exactly where to find them, in the outhouse."

And true to his word, half an hour later, he returned with an armful of old newspapers. He plonked them down on a clearing on top of the old varnished dining table and left me to it.

"I'd better get to school, before the pupils start smashing up the classroom."

"Thanks Unc, I'll see you later."

The old newspapers smelt fusty, not at all dissimilar to the inside of grandpa's wardrobe where Nana still kept his old clothes. This might be a family curse, I thought, not being able to throw things away. I couldn't imagine ever getting rid of any of my vinyl records.

I rubbed my hands together and apart from a thin coating of dust on the spines of these old copies of the Craven Times, they were still in remarkable condition and easily readable. I flicked through the earlier issues, until I came to Friday, September 20th – 'Local Miners win grievance against the mine owners by holding a sit in for three days at the bottom of a pit'. Interesting, but not what I was looking for. Below the headline story, I also noticed an article about how Skipton would soon be going smokeless to protect the environment, commencing at the posh end of town, typical.

Moving on to the following week, I found my story.

Friday, September 27th – 'Girl, 11 found dead'. There didn't seem to be much sentiment wasted in the title. Reading on, the article described how a girl had left her school at lunchtime, feeling unwell. She had collected her younger sister from the infants and had gone home. Her younger sister, Max, was found in a distraught state by the children's mother, when she returned home at around five p.m. The eleven year old's body was discovered in the child's bedroom, an empty jar of pain killers beside her. She was later taken to Bradford Victoria hospital, where a post mortem was carried out to establish the cause of death. A police spokesman had added that they were not treating her death as suspicious at this stage and would not be pursuing anyone else in connection with what appeared to be no more than a tragic suicide. There was on old, black and white school photograph taken of Kate's junior school class at St. Johns in Carleton. Her face had been ringed by the Craven Times to indicate who she was. I brought the photo up closer to get a more detailed look at her features, but it was too small to see any family resemblance with Max.

I picked up Kate's diary again, its sad contents now lost in time. What a pity it hadn't been found during the initial investigation. But even now, in 1977, who would believe a child's scribblings over that of a parent? Back then Kate was convinced that no one would believe what was happening between her and her father. He was too clever for that. The more I thought about it, the more I thought Kate and Max's father had got away with it. All the years of abuse, even if he was still alive, or even if I could track him down, what would be the outcome now?

But Kate and Max deserved a better outcome than the one they had chosen for themselves. Part of me was saying confront the bastard. Shake him up. Let him know he had to answer for his crimes. Maybe he's remarried and has a newer family. What if his children were in danger right now? My thoughts were running away with themselves, but I just couldn't let it go. I thought, at the very least, I could take the bus up to Farley tomorrow and have a poke around, just to satisfy my need to do something for Max and Kate.

Around the middle of the afternoon, I popped into town to see mum at her fashion shop to ask her advice about what to wear for Saturday's wedding. I was in luck she said. "We've just had a delivery of some new, men's linen suits." Trying them on in front of mum and her shop assistants turned into a fashion parade and I was the mobile mannequin. It was embarrassing. Eventually, by popular approval, I chose a pale blue, three piece number, with an orange, paisley patterned shirt and matching tie. By the end of the afternoon, in truth, I was past caring, but I had to admit when I got my purchases back to Uncle Ray's and tried them on again in front of the bedroom mirror, my new clothes did look a 'knock out'.

When Uncle Ray returned home, he'd a fresh pile of school textbooks under his arm. The dining room table was still covered in the old copies of the Craven Times, exactly as I'd left them. Top of the pile was still the one from September 27th 1963.

He glanced down at the headline and frowned. "So this is what you're interested in, a young girls suicide? I knew her slightly," he admitted. "She was one of my first year students. Quiet lass. Came as a shock to us all in the staff room at the time. Not the sort of thing you ever forget in a hurry."

"The newspaper says she took an overdose. She must have been very unhappy." But there was nothing Uncle Ray could tell me that I hadn't already learnt by reading the article in the Craven Times. I went into the kitchen as Uncle Ray continued to talk.

"She'd only been at school a month or so, not long enough to make an assessment of her, or even get to meet her parents at the end of term parents' evening. So tell me, what's your interest in her?" he asked, taking the mug of tea from my hand. "Thanks Mark."

I sat down again at the dining table opposite Uncle Ray.

"I knew her sister. She died last year. She," I felt a lump in my throat, "committed suicide too."

"Dearie me, that's awful. Did you know her well?"

"You could say that. She was my girlfriend."

I gave Uncle Ray the shortened version of how we met, that we worked together and spent most of last summer in each other's company. I mentioned about the newspaper article in the Craven Times and what a pity it was that the photo wasn't clear enough to tell if Kate resembled Max.

"I might be able to help you there," he said confidently. "Every year, most school kids used to have their portraits taken at Christmas, to give to the relatives as presents. It helped to raise money for their school. The photographer is a chap called Perry Thornton. He still has a studio shop on Broughton Road. I'd give him a try. He used to do all the local junior schools."

I asked Uncle Ray if he fancied popping into town later for a drink. "Sorry Mark, I've a lot of marking to catch up on. But if you're looking for your dad, he's usually in the Spread Eagle."

The high street in Skipton dated back to the days of the Magna Carta, when the right to hold a free market place had been granted. The reserved spaces for the market stalls still dominated the look of the town. Large, cobbled sidings flanked both sides of the high street. They were wide enough for the many, modern canopied stalls that were erected almost daily from Monday to Saturday. Beyond the cobblestones and in front of the many Victorian fronted, retail shops was a wide, stone flagged pavement. It wasn't paved in gold, but you could smell the colour of money as you walked along it. Skipton was doing very well for itself. And right now it was looking even more friendly and prosperous. As part of the Silver Jubilee celebrations, row after row of colourful, patriotic bunting draped across the high street, in readiness to welcome Her Majesty. Even the shop windows displayed framed portraits of our smiling Queen, alongside all sorts of commemorative souvenirs: plates, mugs, plaques, coins and medals, even silver jubilee pet products.

Squeezed between the iron colonnaded shops and on both sides of the street were half a dozen pubs and hotels. At the bottom of the high street was a busy junction and at the top of town the road forked immediately in front of the medieval castle gates. The Spread Eagle was at the top end of town just inside the left fork of Gargrave Road and just a ten minute walk from Uncle Ray's.

Dad was in his customary position, propping up the bar and was having a chinwag with the publican about the state of the nation.

"Here, try one of these lad," he said, handing me a pint of Timothy Taylors. "This'll put hairs on your chest." Dad was always pleased to see me and always proud to show me off to strangers. It was just his way, even if I did find it embarrassing. "Just back from the south of France, crewing aboard a big yacht," he boasted for anyone to hear.

"Cheers dad. I see you've found your new home," I said cheekily.

"I'll say this for the Yorkies, they know how to brew a decent pint. Mind you they still know nowt about cricket."

"I heard that," interrupted the publican.

"Come on, let's sit down and you can tell me all about your adventures."

Being early evening, the pub was still quiet. There were only a few straggling souls, market traders having one for the road before departing, once again, with their vans and their wares.

I gave dad the brief highlights of the last four months on the Cote d'Azur: fixing a V8 speedboat engine, learning to water ski and how I'd met some of the Formula One racing drivers. I wasn't sure I should tell him about my heroics during the sinking of the Liberty Princess, so I played down my role in the drama, just in case he thought I was being put at too much risk.

"I was half expecting you to have married a rich princess," he joked. "That Prince Rainier fella, who's married to Grace Kelly, has a couple of eligible daughters. Should be right up your street," he laughed, half seriously.

"I'm just concentrating on my job at the moment and having a bit of fun too at the same time."

"I don't blame you lad. These are the best days of your life, make the most of them," and he slapped me on the shoulder for good measure. "So what's next, son?"

"I'm not sure. I haven't made up my mind yet."

"Well, before you leave make sure you give your mum a big hug. I know she can sound a bit mean at times, but that's just because she worries so much about you. She loves you to bits. All I'm trying to say is there's no need to hang around here on our account. Your mother and me will be alright, once we find a place of our own. If I were in your boots son, I'd be off like a shot. You gotta enjoy yersen while you're young."

I couldn't argue with him there. Once I'd drawn a line under Max and Kate's death, then maybe I'd see my future in a clearer way.

The next morning and not for the first time since I'd returned home to England, it was chucking it down. The rainwater was running down the gutter in torrents as I walked along Broughton Road, looking out for the photographer's studio, which Uncle Ray had put me onto. I soon came across a small window with a faded, crimson coloured velvet curtain. Centre stage was a framed photograph of a young girl, who looked around four years old, with crooked teeth and a cute smile. Languishing on a shelf below was a dusty collection of old cameras and above the curtain was a notice which read:
Peregrine Thornton
Family portraits, Christenings and Weddings
'Watch the Birdie'

The hanging doorbell shook as the entrance door freed itself from the tight grip of the frame as I pushed it open and shook off the rain like a longhaired dog. Behind the door curtain that faced me, I heard a few grumbles, as the person behind it tried to find the opening. Then, a flustered, bespectacled face popped out through the gap. As soon as he saw he had a customer, he bade me a friendly good morning.

"Nice day for ducks," he said in his squeaky voice.

I introduced myself as the nephew of Raymond Crabtree and asked if it was possible to obtain a copy of Kate Ried's portrait from 1962. "She was in the top class at St. Johns in Carleton." He appeared to be impressed with my knowledgeable enquiry, but I sensed he was having second thoughts. He may have looked like an old eccentric, but he was no push over. He reminded me of someone.

"Are you a relative of Miss Ried?"

"No, just a family friend. I'll be visiting her mother in Crowston at the weekend. I thought it would be a nice keepsake for her." I felt myself blush at telling a white lie, but I'd not really thought through beforehand what I was going to say.

"Crowston you say," rubbing his chin. "Not many pubs there."

"No, there aren't any, just three churches." The old beggar was testing me, I thought. Perry smiled back at me and relaxed his shoulders as if I'd just given him the answer to a secret password.

"Well, okay. Pop back tomorrow and I'll have it ready for you. It'll be ten shillings. Sorry, I mean fifty pence. I was back in 1962 for the minute there."

As I stood in the bus shelter opposite, waiting for my transportation to Farley, I knew I'd need to be better prepared with what I was going to say if I was to confront Max and Kate's father. But what if he didn't live there anymore? Well I'd come this far. There didn't seem to be any point in turning back now. Besides, he was probably none the wiser about Max's suicide and that was the point I wanted to drive home between his eyes: how he'd driven both his daughters to their deaths.

It was a steady climb out of Skipton up onto the heath. Inside of the old Skipton and Craven bus, all the windows were thickly steamed up. It made little difference when I wiped them. The dirt and the arrows of raindrops on the outside made it impossible for me to see through them anyway. I had no idea where I was heading. Instead, I watched the back of the driver as he grappled with the large steering wheel and stirred the long lever whilst he crashed through the gears. The complaining tone of the engine seemed to say, 'Here we go again', then the sound of the gears, urgh, urgh crash - change down. 'Here we go again', urgh, urgh crash - change down. At every cattle grid crossing the contemptible old bus rattled and trembled, but without the slightest care. No doubt, It had survived this daily occurrence a thousand times before. It was just me who was feeling apprehensive about the outcome of the journey.

The tiny village of Farley was, as Ray had beautifully described, bleak. It looked even darker and more brooding inside the current, grey, rain soaked cloud. As I watched my lifeline on four wheels disappear through the mist, I became aware I was the only person to have disembarked here.

On one side of the street there was a dirty old farmyard. Muddied tractor tracks ran back and forth and up the centre of the street. The farm was dominated by a long, stone barn which had no windows, just a wooden, arched door, bolted tightly to. On the opposite side of the street was a jagged row of cottages with their noses up against the kerb. Their windows were layered with muck and dust and were still dressed in the same impoverished clothes of their doomed abandonment; hessian potato sacks for curtains, whose torn, ragged hems were woven into cobwebs. It was a depressing place. Surely, these houses must be deserted.

So this had to be Wood End, there was no other street name. I began walking up the street in the direction of the church and a faint scratching sound. I counted down the consecutive pairs of numbers from fourteen. The scratching sound was getting louder. When I reached number four I saw an old woman bent down on her knees, polishing her front step with a donkey stone. I paused beside the gap where her front gate had once hung and she turned around. She looked as stony and worn out as the step she was polishing. She cupped a hand to her ear. Through her open front door the interior of the house was uncarpeted.

"Does Mister Ried still live next door?" I asked.

"Aye he does."

"Do you know if he's at home?"

"Aye, I reckon. He never goes out." I glanced at the house next door. Just protruding from the edge of the gable end I could see a parked car, a new, yellow Ford Escort. I turned to thank the old lady, but she'd already vanished behind her closed door. I looked at the shiny new car again and thought perhaps this Mister Ried has got himself remarried. It was just a thought for the sake of steadying my nerves. I was attempting to add some kind of normality to this creepy environment. I went and stood in front of the door at number two and knocked twice. I clenched my fists inside my coat pockets and held my head as high as I could, ready to face him.

The door was opened, to my surprise and some relief, by a friendly looking nurse.

"Is Mister Ried at home?" I asked.

"Yes come in out of the drizzle, love. What name is it?"

"Most people just call me Byrney."

She led me through to the back room and as she opened the bare wooden door I was struck by a blast of stuffy heat.

"You have a visitor, John," she said pleasantly. I followed behind her further, into the hot, dimly lit room, but before I reached the hearth I stopped suddenly. I was totally unprepared for what confronted me. Next to the open fireplace was a pathetic creature, slumped in a wheel chair. His head was caged inside a steel wire bridle, which also had a fixed metal spoon that disappeared into his mouth.

"Is this Mister Ried?"

"Yes, don't let his appearance worry you. He's paralysed from the neck down. He can't speak, but he can see and hear very well.

"This is Byrney," said the kindly nurse, catching Ried's attention. Seeing him in such a ghastly predicament had completely thrown me. The angry speech I'd been saying to myself during my journey up here was now lost.

"How long has he been like this?" I said turning to face the nurse once more.

"Ever since the car accident. He had a head on collision about seven years ago. I think his family had deserted him a few years before that too, poor thing. But at least he has me to look after him. How do you know him, Byrney?"

"I don't really," I confessed. "I was a friend of his daughter."

"You mean the one who killed herself?"

I realised we were at cross-purposes. She thought I meant Kate, when actually I was talking about Max. I didn't correct her. I didn't reply at all, I just looked down at Ried.

"Would you like a cup of tea?" she asked.

"No thanks. I have to be getting along. I just came to give Mister Ried something." Then I took out Kate's diary from my pocket. I looked at Ried again and I thought I detected a little agitation in his eyes. "This was his daughter's diary. I found it recently and I thought he might like to have it as a memento.

"I'm sure he would," replied the nurse, gratefully accepting the gift on Ried's behalf.

Then I looked at Ried defiantly, eye to eye, and suggested what a lovely idea it would be if she read it out loud to him, page by page. Maybe the memories would come flooding back.

"That's a splendid idea. How thoughtful."

When I left the sad, stifling, stale old house I understood how my old friend Gastin De Bourges felt, ticking off the names on his wanted list, when his quarry was finally made to face the music. I hoped that my actions today would be the silver bullet that Ried had managed to dodge his whole life. One thing was certain; sooner or later he would be made to pay. If not in a court of law then at least the one last friendly face he had left in the world would know the truth of who he was.

When I reached the bus stop at the top of the village, I carried on walking. The stone parish church was directly in font of me. There was something drawing me towards it, something

vaguely familiar. Could history be repeating itself again? I had
an urgent need to check out the small graveyard. It would only
take five more minutes.

It didn't even take me that long to find the grave I was
looking for. A black marble headstone with gold lettering;

Kate Ried
Born 26th November 1951
Died 24th September 1963
Rest In Peace

So it wasn't a random coincidence, after all, that Max had
ended her life on the day of Eve's funeral. It was the exact same
day of the year as Kate had chosen. Having already seen the
same date on Max's headstone, seeing it on Kate's too sent a
sad shiver down my spine. So I wasn't to blame. I felt an
overwhelming sense of relief. If only I'd known about Kate
before Max's death, but how could I have.

I took shelter in the arched porch-way as a shower passed
overhead. The internal walls were lined with ancient,
gravestone lids, weathered beyond any decipher. There was an
honesty box screwed down onto a wooden sill. It displayed
copies of a potted history of St. Michael's Parish Church,
Farley-in-Craven. According to the pamphlet, the entrance
porch in whose shelter I was sat dated back to 1198,
unmistakably Norman in it's origin.

It was long after school closing time when I returned to
Mount Pleasant Villas. Uncle Ray was just mopping up his egg
yolk with half a slice of buttered white bread.

"I'd given you up. The kettle's just boiled if you want to
make yourself a brew."

"Would you like one Unc?"

"Might as well, if you're making one."

I went through the events of my day with Uncle Ray. My
visit to Thornton's photography studio and the bus ride up to
Farley.

"Miserable place. They must be a hardened lot to stick it out in that god forsaken hole," he quipped. I couldn't disagree with him. My mind was still focussed on Kate, lying up there. As for Ried, I hoped he'd soon be making headlines in the Craven Times.

"The old parish church is very interesting," I said. "Dates back to Norman times. Even has a Norman arched porch to prove it."

"I wouldn't be at all surprised to learn that there was an even older place of worship beneath those stones. If ever a lonely village needed a place of worship, it was Farley," suggested Ray.

I understood what he meant. During the afternoon, I'd had an eerie feeling all the time I'd been there. Even when the sun had briefly shone through the clouds, I'd still felt chilled. I was glad to leave.

There was still one more unexpected, shocking discovery to unearth the next day when I returned to Perry Thornton's studio. The photograph I'd ordered threw a whole different complexion on Kate's story. When Perry handed me the portrait of Kate from 1962, the only answer to putting two and two together - was pure dynamite, pure tragic dynamite. I couldn't stop staring at the striking, coloured features of this innocent, eleven year old girl. And knowing the revelations they would unleash made me feel incredibly sad.

"Is everything alright?" Asked Perry

"Perfect, thank you. This is Kate Ried?" I asked just wanting to make sure.

"Yes, check the reverse. I might look a bit fuzzy but I can still read."

I turned over the reverse side of the coloured photograph and noticed the faded ink date stamp in the middle: 15 Dec 1962. And in hand written pencil: St. Johns, Class 1 - Kate Ried.

Perry's given me his original copy, I thought.

"It's fifty 'p' isn't it, you said?"

Perry rested his elbows on the counter and dropped his long chin inside his framed hands. "As you're a relative of Ray Crabtree's, you can have it for nothing," And with a lopsided grin, he pushed the coloured photo across the counter.

"Thank you very much." I slid the photo back inside the white envelope and placed it carefully inside my breast pocket, said goodbye and stepped back out, into the warm sunshine on Broughton Road.

Chapter Ten

Wedding

The last time I'd been knocking at the door of number 9, Grant Road, I'd just returned from climbing to the top of Ingleborough Hill, the very birthplace of my adventures. It's funny how our ideas are born. If I'd not gone to the trouble of taking Eve's ashes to the top of the Pyrenees, I know for sure, I wouldn't be the same person as I am right now. Being in control of my own destiny, the path I'd chosen for myself back then, had also put me at the hub of colliding with or being touched by situations which were out of my control. So much had changed in these past nine months. Mostly these were changes I felt inside of me: an inner strength, a confidence I could rely on and the simple fact I'd learnt how not to be afraid of having a go. As a result of all these, I'd discovered I could influence and alter the course of situations which were alien to the boy I once was. And yet I still had wobbles of anxiety and I felt there was something gnawing at me. Some kind of a growing emptiness - a hunger in my soul, which needed to be nourished… Whatever was at the heart of it was most likely staring straight at my face, but I was too caught up in myself to notice. But now was not the time to delve any further. By this time tomorrow Kevin and Vicky would be getting hitched and I was determined to enjoy every moment.

Kevin was the first of my mates to take this brave step and I admired him for it. He was a likeable, mature guy with ambitions and he'd also won the heart of probably the prettiest girl in Crowston. He'd played an open hand, right from that first day he'd started working at the Friary, nothing fancy, just friendly and determined, with a natural gift for carrying

everyone along with him. Not bad for a Blackpool fan, I
thought.

When the door opened it was Fionn's mum, who
immediately pounced on me. So that was where Fionn gets it
from. Her mum had her hands clasped to my arms and was
kissing my cheeks.

"Fionn's told me all about your heroics at sea, you're so
brave. But most of all I want to thank you for looking after my
little girl and bringing her home safe."

I didn't know what to say. It was Fionn who came to my
rescue.

"For heavens sake, mum. Let go of Byrney, you're being
embarrassing."

Mrs. Terry winked at me. "I love it when I make her feel
embarrassed," she teased, as she led me into their home and
closed the door.

After a lovely, summery meal inside their cosy conservatory
I felt a little ungrateful at having to dash off so soon. I
apologised and explained that I'd an important errand to run
which would take me an hour or two.

There was a knock on the spare bedroom door where I was
camped for the weekend - it was Fionn. I could tell she wasn't
pleased.

"I suppose you're going up to the Star, aren't you?"

"Yer sorry, I have to. I've got some news for Julie, which I
think she'll want to hear. Come with me if you like?"

"What news are you talking about?"

I sensed Fionn was maybe thinking I was becoming
romantically involved, but I couldn't explain myself to her in
any great detail, until I'd first spoken to Julie.

"Fionn, listen to me, there's nothing going on between me
and Julie. It's not like that at all." I was hoping to reassure
Fionn. The last thing I wanted to do was upset her. "It has
something to do with Max's suicide. I promise I'll tell you
everything later, as soon as I get back. There's still time for you
to change your mind" I pulled a funny face.

"It's okay, you go. Besides I've stuff to do for the wedding. I need to do my nails, see." She held out her chipped digits.

"Err yer, I see what you mean," I laughed.

It was comforting to be sat, once more, on a red, double decker bus bound for Lancaster, passing the old, familiar landmarks: Ossie's garage, the disused lorry park, and opposite, the ruins of the old hotel. Despite their dilapidated state, they all had a sense of permanence about them. Even the smell of the old leather bench seats and the cigarette ash, as dirty and as overbearing as they were, couldn't dispel the thought that here I was, bouncing along back home in West Lancashire and how good it felt to be here. Beneath the window someone had scribbled, 'Seasiders Rule'.

And here, sat in my favourite position on the front seat, on the top deck, was living proof that old habits die hard. I still had to be the first to see what was coming up around the next bend. Affording myself the longest possible time to prepare for what lay ahead.

First, there was another big embrace to deal with, this time from Julie who was waiting for me in the plush surroundings of the lounge bar at the Star Inn. If things carried on like this, I wasn't sure my neck was going to get through the weekend, What with all the people I'd likely be meeting up with whom I'd not seen since last October.

There were two welcoming pints of Guinness already on our table. We exchanged pleasantries and briefly spoke about our time in the south of France and of course our daring rescue aboard the burning Liberty Princess. The details were still fresh in our memories.

When our pints were half full Julie started listening to me more intently as I began telling her about what I'd learnt from Kate's diary.

"Have you got it with you? I'd like to read it for myself. I can't believe Max's father was that sort. He was always kind whenever I saw him." Then the look on Julie's face suddenly changed. "I'd like to give him a piece of my mind now though, the evil bastard."

"It wouldn't do any good."

"Why, is he dead? Death would be too easy an escape for the likes of him."

I started to smile a little. "Then you have your wish there." And I went on to explain about my recent visit to his home and how I'd stitched him up for good. And that there wasn't a single thing he could do about it.

This brought the biggest smile I'd seen from Julie and then she laughed out loud, one of her horsey guffaws. "My god, well done, Byrney. I'd love to see him squirm when his nurse reads out Kate's diary to him."

It was impossible not to join in with her laughter, despite knowing that the next part of my story would bring her crashing back down to earth. I was still wondering how to break the rest of my news to her. I scratched the back of my neck for inspiration.

"There's more, isn't there?" She'd been reading my body language. "What aren't you telling me?"

I took a deep breath. "It's about Kate." I said, looking straight into Julie's green eyes. I detected for the first time Julie had a vulnerable side to her bravado.

"There's an old stone church at Farley, a sad looking place. That's where I found Kate's grave. You should go there for a visit, when you feel up to it. The church dates back to Norman times."

"What do you mean by, when I feel up to it?"

I put my hand in my breast pocket and took out the white envelope.

"What's this?" The suspense was beginning to get to her.

"It's a school photo of Kate, taken just before she died."

I picked up my drink and swallowed what was left in the glass as Julie removed the photo from the envelope. She was looking at the reverse side to begin with; then she turned it over. I'd been trying to anticipate her reaction ever since I'd first seen Kate's colour portrait. I saw Julie's puzzled look. She was trying to figure it out, whilst holding back her tears. Kate's portrait could have passed for Julie herself, as an eleven year old. They were almost identical. The exact same red hair and green eyes that only a coloured photograph could have revealed. There was absolutely no doubt as to whom Kate's father was - it was Lord Nugent.

Julie burst into tears and stood up. She kept apologising. "Sorry, I have to go," she cried. "I have to go." She was in floods of tears as she scrambled away from our table. Seeing how distressed she was, I was holding back my own emotions too.

I sat there for a further fifteen minutes, staring into the space of Julie's empty seat, contemplating the tragedy of it all. I knew it would hit her hard. All her life she'd believed she'd been an only child. Max had been her friend since childhood. And Max too would most likely never have known that her sister Kate was also Julie's half sister. "What a fucking mess," I said to myself.

Back at Cayburn an hour later, I was retelling the full, sorrowful tale to Fionn and her mum. They were both shocked too and not surprisingly, they both felt incredibly sorry for Julie. Lost for words, we all called time on an early night - 'tomorrow's another day'. It was the only consolation.

I was stood in the shade on the patio, with a mug of tea. The day had obviously been warming up since dawn and already the temperature felt sultry, not a single breath of a breeze anywhere. Having showered after breakfast, I was now waiting in my new togs, minus the jacket, which was flung over the back of a chair. If the temperature kept on rising like this, it was going to be one 'helluva' sweltering and thirsty day. I waited for Fionn to make an appearance. She'd been out of the house this morning before I'd even got up, out to the hairdresser in town.

I stood watching the birds and the bees come and go in the garden. I was trying to work out why I was feeling so nervous. Maybe I was feeling nervous about meeting a lot of people whom I'd not seen for a long time, maybe. Maybe I was feeling nervous for Kevin and Vicky, nervous for their day. Any of these reasons would have been better than what was actually making me feel nervous - seeing Fionn all dressed up in her new outfit, her new hairdo and polished nails - 'This is just daft', I told myself.

I could hear Fionn talking to her mum in the kitchen and her mum telling her I was out on the patio.

When Fionn stepped out of the back door, she looked amazing. Her smile and make up exaggerated the size and loveliness of her eyes. I was almost bowled over.

"Well, how do I look?" she asked, doing a flamenco twirl which made her dress fan out. Her floaty, patterned, mauve coloured dress I could see was tied behind her neck and her back was completely bare, showing off her Mediterranean tan. I noticed for the first time how her shoulders and the tops of her arms were dappled with freckles. She also had on the most outrageously high platform shoes too, which made her appear at least an inch taller than me.

"Well?" she asked again. "It's a halter neck dress from Chelsea Girl in Lancaster. I bought it my first day back, specially for today."

I felt myself blush up. The beautiful, mature woman, which Fionn had become, was unrecognisable from the scruffy, funny girl that I'd always known since infant school and all I could say was, "you've scrubbed up nicely."

"You're not half bad yourself," she replied laughing.

"Actually Fi, joking aside, you look wonderful." I bent forward instinctively and kissed her cheek.

"Make your mind up," she said. "You do realise I have to stand perfectly still all day otherwise everything will fall apart," she joked.

And here's me thinking I'd just been let off the hook, that she hadn't sensed how much faster my heart was beating. "You're safe with me." I replied.

When we arrived in Crowston, it seemed like the whole village had turned out for Kevin and Vicky's wedding. There was festival bunting strung out everywhere. The Union jacks, which were flying, were obviously in celebration of the Queens silver jubilee, but there were home made banners too, hanging from first floor windows, wishing them both luck. All the flowerbeds were freshly dug over and in full bloom with orange marigolds and red peonies. And many of the doorways were framed with overflowing hanging baskets of petunias and trailing lobelia. The ambience was intoxicating. Even the stray cars and cyclists, what few there were, passed through slowly and respectfully. The day was far too hot to go travelling.

The marriage service was due to commence at two p.m. It was just one p.m. when Fionn's mum dropped us at the cobbles outside the Friary.

In front of Madge and Edward's house, the parking space had been cordoned off for the wedding guests to mingle in before taking to their seats inside the church.

Not one to miss a trick, I noticed Edward had also rigged up a drinks cooler, outside in the square and was doing a roaring trade selling glasses of ice cool Robinsons Barley Water and other soft drinks. Fionn's mum wanted to wait with us too, at least until the bride and groom arrived.

"Come on, let's pop into the shop and say hello to Madge and Joanie. I've been dying to see them again," said Fionn excitedly. I followed along and we went through the double doors arm in arm. Joanie was first to spot us.

"Don't you two look a lovely couple," she teased.

"It'll be your turn next. Mark my words," shouted Madge from the top of the kitchen step. "Eee don't they look well together."

"It's this fake tan," I said. "It washes off you know. Need a hand with the dishes?"

"Not today thank you. We've got twenty staff laid on so we'd better be all alright."

Then Edward appeared from the rear corridor. "Well if it isn't Fionn and Byrney," he chortled. "I didn't realise you were getting married too. When's the big day?"

"We'll let you know," replied Fionn.

We stood there chatting for a few more minutes until Madge had to tell Edward to get back outside as there was a queue forming at his cold drinks dispensary.

Half an hour to kick off, we joined Fionn's mum back outside amongst the gathering crowd. She was talking to Glenda, one of the older members of staff at the Friary and fellow wedding guest. Fionn pointed out to me Glenda's husband Jim, who looked a timid soul and was half the size of Glenda in both directions.

"He doesn't say much," whispered Fionn. "It's a well known fact that in a marriage one partner always makes up for what the other one lacks."

"Hence, Glenda's the biggest gas bag in Crowston," I joked.

Just then I saw Kevin's green mini pull up into the square. He got out of the driving seat and took out his top hat from off the back seat. At the same time, a slightly smaller version of himself copied his actions from the passenger side.

Fionn had taken on the role of running commentator. "That's his younger brother, Ian. He was the one trying to chat me up at the Friary Christmas do last year. I couldn't get rid of him."

"I think he'll already have his hands full today. According to Edward, he's Kevin's best man."

Kev saw Fionn waving at him and he made his way over, shaking various hands as he moved closer.

"Hey up guys, good to see you both made it."

"Aren't you nervous?" asked Fionn

"Yes, a bit, but it doesn't matter. Even if I fluff my lines, it's going to be a fantastic day no matter what."

"Hey, I think we ought to be making a move," I said checking my watch.

"Do you mind if we wait here Byrney, I want to see Vicky arrive too?" asked Fionn, struggling to contain her excitement again.

Kevin headed off up towards the church, catching up with his best man. "Good luck mate," I called after him.

After a few more minutes, we could hear people clapping from higher up the main street, and the sound of the approaching horse's hooves. We faced the square as an open topped carriage came into view, with Vicky and her three sisters as bridesmaids sat inside. Vicky was waving at everyone like the Queen of England. It was an incredible sight. A crowd of villagers were following behind on foot, still clapping and smiling in the bright afternoon sunshine. It appeared they'd just been carried along, stuck in the excitement of the moment. There were more flowers and white ribbons decorating the horse as well as the carriage. Fionn took out her camera from her clasp bag and snapped away as the procession slowly came to a halt, in front of St.Mary's church.

As the bride and bridesmaids dismounted and began to straighten their trains into line, we slipped past them, Fionn waving and shouting "Good luck, honey."

"Lovely to see you," replied Vicky coolly blowing her a kiss. She didn't sound the least bit nervous either.

It was strikingly obvious that there was always something very calming about Kevin and Vicky whenever they were together. I remember being sat next to them on a few occasions at the Star and I just knew instantly that they were meant for one another. They were such a content and balanced couple.

"Come on, we have to get inside before Vicky," I said as Fionn kissed her mum with a 'see you later'.

"I think she'll still be here when we come out again," she commented.

We squeezed in at the back of the church, in the last two, remaining empty places amongst the pews. Still, at least we'd be able to hear them, even if we couldn't see them clearly. The organ began to play the wedding march and after the first opening bar, the congregation fell silent and shuffled to their feet looking behind them to get a glimpse of the bride and her entourage. As Vicky glided past, smiling under her veil, I felt Fionn squeeze my arm. Inside the cool and decorative and majestic house of God, I absorbed everything that was happening. I'd not experienced anything like this before. This was such a special time. I felt so grown up and so happy to be a part of it. The romance was somehow totally infectious. Everyone inside the church was smiling and holding hands.

It was great too, being sat at the back observing the full panorama of events: the vicar issuing his ceremonial words in a serious tone, the wedding group stood perfectly still, the children fidgeting on the hard wooden seats, mums, dads aunts and uncles, friends and relatives, all craning to hear the bride and grooms responses. When they each said 'I do' Fionn and I looked at one another for a second.

"I'm so proud of them," she whispered.

"Yer, me too," I said softly.

There were a few raucous cheers when Kevin kissed his bride and we at the back clapped our hands in approval. It was not a short kiss.

Then they walked out, hand in hand, into the chaos of the waiting crowds and the orchestration of photos - so many cameras - there were hundreds of them. When the official one's were herded up we asked the photographer to take one of just the two of us. "It'll be a nice surprise for them," we giggled.

As expected, the Friary provided the catering for the wedding banquet. After all, it was the only eatery in Crowston. However, it wasn't being held inside the restaurant. Instead, a dining area had been set up specially, in the orchard, out in the back garden. Unfortunately, the only access was across the backyard. At least all the empty cardboard boxes had been bailed up, I observed. We walked past the big hut where the pop bottles were stored. The same hut that I'd painfully helped to shift over a year ago. Amazingly, it was still intact and in the same place where we'd left it.

The rest of the garden was unrecognisable. Edward had organised a couple of his tractor boys to tidy up, by trimming the fruit trees and cutting the grass. Beneath each tree there was an old wooden barrel which had three planks of oak nailed down on top of it to form a rustic table. The seating was made up of fresh bales of hay. At the stage end of the garden, a canvas canopy had been installed and a longer version of our table, utilising four barrels, had been rigged up to form one long table for the main wedding party. It had the same seating arrangement too - bales of hay, all strung together. It was such a simple plan, which functioned perfectly and looked wonderfully old fashioned.

"It's like a scene from a Thomas Hardy novel," enthralled Fionn. "He's so clever, is Edward."

"I think Kevin and Vicky might have had something to do with it too. I don't think Ned's this artistic. He's just a Wurzel at heart."

"Well I don't care, it looks wonderful."

Fionn was right. The organisation that had gone into creating this day hadn't just happened by chance. Everybody had contributed something and no one wanted to miss it.

By eight o' clock, Fionn said she'd had enough to drink.

"Shall we go for a walk?" I suggested.

We strolled through the village, tracing our footsteps from earlier in the day and without realising we'd found our way back to the churchyard and were stood in front of Max's headstone.

"That date will always haunt me," I said.

"Then you'll have to do something really nice on it this year instead," said Fionn brashly. I could tell she'd been drinking. Then she removed her buttonhole flower and placed it gently at her feet on Max's grave.

"What do you think Max would have reckoned to all this?" I asked, "The wedding, the village and everything? Do you think she'd have been happy?"

"Whenever I think of Max now, it's funny but, I always seem to picture Magenta," replied Fionn. "They're similar personalities."

"Yer, I noticed that too. Different looks, but very much alike in their actions."

I liked listening to Fionn's philosophy. She had a way of keeping things in perspective, of keeping things moving forward in life. I also had a feeling she'd been shaping up to ask me something important too. Something we'd both avoided discussing so far.

"All this talk about work, I've told my mum I'm going back to France tomorrow."

"I always knew that's what you wanted," I said, automatically.

Whilst I'd been staring at Max's headstone, Fionn had moved up close to me. I hadn't noticed she'd also put a hand on my shoulder. "What about you then?"

"Would you be angry if I didn't come with you?"

She pulled her hand away. "Angry? Of course not, disappointed, yes, definitely. But it wouldn't stop me from leaving." Fionn didn't show the slightest emotion.

"Good, I wouldn't want it to." I locked my arm with hers and suggested we get back to the wedding for a little while longer.

It was impossible to be angry with one another. It was like we'd both been travelling down the same road together all our lives and suddenly the road had narrowed down to just a single track, just wide enough for one person and one of us was going to have to give way. I wasn't going to be the bully and force Fionn into doing what I wanted. I'd seen a lot of lads forcing their girlfriends into accepting that the man was in charge. It always felt an uncomfortable and unnatural way to behave to me. In my mind, a boy and girl partnership should be on equal terms. And a girl should be allowed to flower into the kind of woman she wanted to be. I didn't want Fionn making any sacrifices on account of me.

The village hall was practically shaking on its foundations; there were so many people inside. All the staff at the Friary had come up straight from work at the end of their shifts. Most of them had come prepared with an extra set of clothes to change into and a young man to accompany them. Amongst the waitresses was Janet Johnson, who was still going out with my old mate Lewis. It wasn't long before I saw him arrive on his new, monster, two-wheeled machine - a Kawasaki Z900. I was so envious.

"Hey up mate, wasn't expecting to see you here. How's things?"

"Yer, good thanks. Passed my test a couple of weeks ago and bought this brute straight from Poulton Motorcycles. Just picked it up earlier - goes like shit off a shovel."

It was great to see him again. He was telling me about his recent trip to the Isle of Man to watch the TT Races. "Brilliant Byrney, you'd have loved it. There were thousands of bikes there. The racing was out of this world. We were stood near Ballaugh Bridge, where the bikes take off the ground. Good pub there an' all." I told Lewis about meeting some of the F1 drivers on our yacht.

"F1's for girls. Bikes are for real daredevils. Remember them Byrney? You used to be one of us." Lewis paused to knock back his pint. "Listen we're all riding down to the Costa Brava next month, why don't you come along?"

"I haven't got a bike," I said lamely.

"I'll lend you my old KH250 triple."

Mention of this particular model of bike suddenly brought a memory back into view, a wet winter evening, straight from school when the four of us had ridden into Blackpool on our mopeds, John, Andy, Lewis and me. We'd stopped off at the bike showroom, near the traffic lights at Poulton. Everyone agreed that night; the KH250 was the best thing ever. And I was now being offered the chance to ride one all the way down to Spain and back. It appealed to my sense of adventure and much safer, I thought, than risking my life aboard a leaky old vessel across the Atlantic.

After a couple more jars with Lewis I went looking for Fionn. We'd agreed to stay on one more hour, and that was an hour and a half ago. I found her just in time to see Kevin and Vicky wave their farewells to the congregation. They'd changed into their travel clothes and were being taxied all the way to Manchester airport for a weeks honeymoon in Tenerife.

Fionn said she was going to call it a night too. We walked outside together to find there were several taxi's waiting to ferry the wedding guests back to their homes. Such a well organised do, I thought. By now we were both happily the worse for wear and not quite looking as good as we had done at the start of the day. My suit trousers were looking grubby and I'd lost my tie. Fionn was more or less still intact but she'd shrunk several inches as she stepped bare foot into the taxi, with her platform shoes in her hands.

We hutched up together on the back seat and rested our spinning heads. "Such a wonderful day," she said, with barely enough energy left to speak, "Such a wonderful day."

When Fionn came to say goodbye to her mum the next morning, the heartache between them was palpable. Stood in the background I was made aware of what a painful worry it is being a mum. I suddenly felt guilty about being insensitive to my own mum's feelings. I was always so caught up in myself: what I wanted, how I wanted to live my life. I could have spared my mum a good deal of anguish had I the courage to say, I love you mum. Nevertheless, I had felt it and maybe mum had recognised that in me, even if she didn't hear it straight from my lips. I'd let my own embarrassment get in the way as usual. That's not how a hero behaves. I saw how Fionn hung onto her mum and visa versa and I felt humbled.

"Don't worry Mrs T. I'll see that Fionn gets off okay."

We travelled down to Preston with nothing much to say to each other. Our ten days off had gone ever so quickly and the time to go our separate ways was hurtling towards us as we reached the central bus station.

"Fi, my bus isn't going for another forty-five minutes. Let me walk you down to the train station."

It's funny, I thought. Here's Fionn heading back to France by herself and she could easily have flown back. But instead she wants to take the Night Ferry train. "It's not always about reaching your destination," she'd said to me earlier. "Sometimes it's about the journey."

I'd been feeling off, ever since I'd woken this morning and it hadn't just been my hangover. There were so many words whizzing round my brain. I thought if I didn't make some sort of decision soon about my future, my head would explode. And it wasn't only words whizzing around. There were visions too, happy ones and some not so happy. I was stuck in limbo and I couldn't see a way out of it. The worse part about it was that I was probably using the sinking of the Princess as an excuse for the way I was thinking. I was letting the coward in me take control again.

We sat side by side on one of the benches outside the waiting room watching the uniforms at work and the suits briskly taking to their seats. When the time came for Fionn to board her train, we looked at one another blankly each of us waiting for the other to say something. The moment seemed frozen. It lingered unmoving, as though time was truly standing still. All the background noise too, had suddenly been made mute. The only voice I heard in my thoughts was my own repeating other people's words back to me.

If I were in your boots, I'd be off like a shot. Best years of your life. Guard your demons Byrney, no good ever comes from dwelling on things. Eee don't they look well together. It'll be your turn next, mark my words. Maybe you're just looking in the wrong places.

"I'm going now Byrney love, wish me luck."

"What? Oh yer, of course."

I let go of Fionn's hand and watched her place her bags on the train and climb in behind them.

I was biting my lip. This was really happening. I was thinking how the decisions we make when we are sixteen, just sixteen years of age have such an impact on the rest of our lives. I'd made the right decision once, a year ago with Eve's ashes and so much had happened to me for the better since then. What was I thinking, now?

I pictured Fionn sat on the train by herself and I knew I couldn't let her go alone. I heard the railway porter's whistle and the sound of the train's engine revving up.

Right now, this was the most decisive moment of my life and I was letting the wrong decision take over. I saw the train start to move. For Gods sake Byrney, what are you waiting for? Don't you love her?

"Bollocks, I really do love her." There wasn't a second to lose and I began to run hard. I knew that if I ran as fast as I could then, maybe, I'd just make it.

"Wait!" I shouted as I tried to catch up. "Stop, wait, I love you!"